DAWN LEE MCKENNA'S

LANDFALL

A *FORGOTTEN COAST* SUSPENSE NOVEL: BOOK FOUR

2015

A SWEET TEA PRESS PUBLICATION

First published in the United States by Sweet Tea Press

Edited by Tammi Labrecque
larksandkatydids.com

Cover by Shayne Rutherford
darkmoongraphics.com

Interior Design by Colleen Sheehan
wdrbookdesign.com

Landfall is a work of fiction. All incidents and dialogue, and all characters, are products of the author's imagination. Any similarities to any person, living or dead, is merely coincidental.

For Chelsey
who is loved

CHAPTER ONE

Maggie laid on the table for two pounding heartbeats, then slid off and onto her feet, and scrambled over to Sky's chair.

"Mom, what just happened?" Sky asked, her voice near hysterical.

"I don't know," Maggie managed to croak, squatting behind Sky's chair and furiously working the ropes that bound her wrists.

"What did he do?"

"I don't know, Sky!"

The wind was whistling like a train outside, and it seemed impossible that it could be louder than it had already been. Maggie looked up toward the kitchen window as something small but hard hit it, and she caught Kyle's eye. He was staring at the front door, his eyes wide.

"I'm coming, Kyle," Maggie said. He looked at her, but didn't say anything.

Sky wiggled her fingers. "Hurry, Mom!"

"Hold still, baby, please," Maggie said.

She yanked the ropes free and jumped up as Sky pulled her arms around to the front. They were stiff from hours of being bound behind her, and she rolled them gingerly.

"Sky," I need you to grab the Glock," Maggie said, as she squatted behind Kyle and started working on the ropes. His thin wrists were bleeding, and the ropes had left welts on them that made Maggie want to scream.

Sky ran over to the kitchen counter and picked up the Glock, where it lay with the Mossberg and her great-grandfather's .38. "Do you want me to bring it to you?"

"No, I need it for you," she said. "Do you remember how to use it?"

"Yeah, but...I guess. Why not the .38?"

"This is not the time for a revolver, baby," Maggie answered. "Just take it. I want you take it, and I want you to take Kyle, and I want you guys to go in my room, and you don't come out unless I come get you."

"Mom, wait—"

"You don't come out unless I come get you, do you understand me?" Maggie yelled.

"Yes."

A branch slammed into the window behind Sky, and she ducked instinctively, but the glass didn't break. The branch fell away again as she straightened up and grabbed the rounds from the counter and shoved them into her pocket.

Maggie finally pulled Kyle's wrists free, and she rubbed them for just a second before she pulled him up from the chair. "Kyle, you go with Sky, and you guys stay in there. Do you hear me?"

"Yeah," he said, his voice a croak.

"Go!" Maggie barked at Sky, and the kids ran down the hallway. As soon as she heard their steps, Coco started barking

and scratching at the door again. Maggie watched Sky open the door, watched the kids go in and slam the door behind them, then she ran over to the kitchen counter.

She glanced up at the front door several times as she loaded the Mossberg, shoved a couple of extra rounds in her shorts pocket, and then ran over to the door. The floor was wet from when he had burst through, and she slipped and nearly went down before catching herself.

She put an ear to the door, but it was a ridiculous thing to do. On the other side was nothing but noise, and she could hear nothing beyond the pounding of the rain on the deck.

She took a deep breath, slammed back the action on the shotgun, and flung open the door.

Boudreaux was in the yard, a few feet from the bottom of the stairs. He was almost knee deep in water from the creek, and the water closest to him was colored a deep, dark red.

He looked up at her, the wind buffeting him and pushing him, his hair whipping wildly.

Maggie raised the shotgun and felt a catch in her throat as she looked into those eyes, so deeply blue even from this distance. She hadn't wanted him to be the one, and she felt, ridiculously, the heaviness of disappointment in her chest.

"I wish you hadn't come here, Mr. Boudreaux."

⚓ ⚓ ⚓

Tuesday, August 11th
8:10am – 28 hours earlier

Her name was Faye. According to the Tallahassee paper, Tropical Storm Faye had visited herself upon Cuba without too much mayhem, but might be upgraded to a Category 1 hurricane in the near future. If so, she was expected to make landfall somewhere between New Orleans and Biloxi.

Bennett Boudreaux set the paper aside, and poured himself another chicory coffee. He'd moved from Houma, LA to Apalachicola, FL decades before Hurricane Katrina, and he still enjoyed a good hurricane. He hoped they'd at least get some nice thunderstorms from Faye as she passed through the Gulf.

Judging by the sunlight streaming through the twelve-pane windows and the French doors that led out to the porch, it wouldn't be today.

Boudreaux ran a hand through his brown hair, still thick and with only a touch of silver above his ears to show his age. At sixty-two, he was youthful and slim, and his deep blue eyes hadn't lost any of their intensity. He smoothed his hair back down and reached for the sugar spoon.

Amelia, Boudreaux's middle-aged Creole cook and housekeeper, stood at the kitchen island, frying one slice of maple bacon in a cast iron skillet.

"I appreciate you don't mess with her none this mornin'," she said to the skillet. "I got to take her over to the hospital for her bone scan in forty-five minutes."

"What's the bone scan for?" Boudreaux asked, stirring pure cane sugar into his coffee.

"Make sure she still got bones," Amelia answered. She used a set of tongs to lift the bacon from the pan and laid it on a small plate next to one over-medium egg and a slice of toast.

Boudreaux watched her, and thought how much more relaxed Amelia seemed since his beloved wife Lily had made her departure for Grand Isle. She'd left three weeks ago, just after the funeral service for his older stepson, Patrick. With any luck, she would find a more appealing husband while she was there. Maybe a more successful crime lord, who took frequent and lengthy trips to Newfound-land.

The French door opened, and Miss Evangeline's aluminum walker clattered through it, with Miss Evangeline herself in tepid pursuit.

Miss Evangeline was Amelia's mother, and Boudreaux's childhood nanny. She was well into her nineties, and often reminded him of a hatchling, tiny and featherless, a creamy yellowish-brown.

Boudreaux got up and walked around to pull out Miss Evangeline's chair as she made her way to the table, the tennis balls on her walker making a soft swish against the hardwood floor.

"Mornin', Mama," Amelia said.

"Mornin', baby," Miss Evangeline answered, her voice like dry palm fronds rubbing together.

Boudreaux waited until Miss Evangeline reached the table, then kissed her on each papery cheek. "Good morning, Miss Evangeline," he said.

"We gon' see," she answered, and got settled into her chair with a great deal of care and precision. Boudreaux walked back to his seat as Amelia set the plate and a cup of tea in front of her mother.

"You need to eat and get on with it," Amelia said. "You still got to change for the doctor."

"Why I got to change?" her mother asked, tilting her Coke-bottle glasses up at her daughter.

"You ain't goin' in that house dress," Amelia said.

"I ain't changin' into somethin' else just so they can tell me to take it off and put on them paper towel."

Amelia heaved out a sigh and walked back to the island. "At least put a sweater on," she said. She took the skillet to the sink and started wiping it out, as Boudreaux opened up the paper again. Miss Evangeline commenced to scrape butter on her toast, staring at the back of the newspaper.

"What in the paper?' she asked.

"Some intellectual giant called in a bomb threat from the customer service phone at a Walmart in Tallahassee, the Governor says we really are making some real headway on drugs, and Tropical Storm Faye is thinking about becoming a Category 1 hurricane."

Miss Evangeline stopped buttering her toast and pushed her glasses back up the bridge of her nose. "I won't have no hurricane comin' round here this flat place, floodin' everything."

"It's not going to flood," Boudreaux said smoothly.

"How you know?" she snapped. "Water come up over here, dump the shark in the yard. I won't tolerate it, me."

"We're too far from the bay," Boudreaux said. "All the sharks will be downtown."

Amelia looked over her shoulder at him from the sink. "I got forty minutes now, to take this woman to the doctor."

Miss Evangeline poked at her lower plate with her little tongue and fastened her magnified eyes on the back of Boudreaux's paper. "You thinkin' it's a good day to sass me some," she said.

Boudreaux lowered his paper and looked at her mildly. "No, I'm just pointing out to you that a little surge from some Cat 1 out in the Gulf isn't going to make it all the way over here to Avenue D."

"You say that now. But when the shark swimmin' all 'round my mango, I ain't gon' put up with it, me. I buzz his face off and make me some gumbo."

"That's a good idea," Boudreaux said, catching Amelia glaring at him. "You stand in your house shoes out there in the flooded yard and start shooting your Taser around."

CHAPTER

The sun was high and blazing over the cemetery when Maggie and Sky got out of the Cherokee and walked across the brittle, late summer grass. There was a decent breeze off the Gulf, and it rattled the fronds of the date and Sabal palms scattered amongst the Live Oaks.

Maggie led Sky over to the headstone at the edge of the nearest section, the simple bouquet of flowers in her hand. They stopped before the small marker. *Grace Carpenter, 1996-2015* was all that was engraved there, and Maggie felt it left so much unsaid.

Back in June, Maggie had shot and killed Grace's boyfriend, a local meth dealer, just as he was about to shoot her. Grace had been trying to help Maggie and Wyatt put Ricky Alessi away, so that she and her young children could have a better, safer life. But Children's Services had taken her children away, and Grace had fluttered into the Gulf from atop the bridge that crossed over to St. George Island. Maggie saw it in her dreams.

"Was she pretty?' Sky asked beside her.

"No," Maggie answered. "But she was beautiful any-way." She laid the bouquet on Grace's grave and straight-ened back up. "You would have liked her, I think, even though you weren't very much alike." She looked over at Sky. "You're tougher than she was; you don't scare easily. She was terrified, but she was brave."

Sky nodded and took a sip of her coffee. "Really sad."

Maggie looked at her daughter's profile a moment. "Sky, I know you're really smart, and you have great friends. But you're almost seventeen. Pretty soon, you'll be off at col-lege, out on your own. Please don't ever fall for some 'bad boy' because you think he's kind of cool."

"Mom. I can barely talk to a guy," Sky said, with a slight eye roll. "Unless we're talking about cars or guns or music, I don't have anything to say."

Sky was right; she had a Victoria's Secret face and body, and the soul of a forty-year old redneck.

"I get that, Sky, but that'll change," Maggie said. "Just be careful. Don't let some guy start controlling you or turn-ing you into something you're not."

"Dude. Not gonna happen," Sky said.

"I'm just saying."

"Me, too." Sky looked at the phone that never left her hand. "It's time to go pick up Wyatt."

Maggie nodded, and looked down at Grace's headstone one more time before turning around to head back to the car. Sky followed.

Halfway back to the Jeep, Maggie looked up and across the cemetery, and saw Bennett Boudreaux standing be-neath a Sabal palm near his son Patrick's grave.

He was a good couple of hundred yards away, but he was standing there with his hands in his trouser pockets, looking right at Maggie. Her steps slowed as their eyes met, an uncomfortable moment, even at that distance. His face was almost blank, unreadable.

"Is that Bennett Boudreaux?" Sky asked beside her.

Maggie broke her gaze from Boudreaux's. "Yes."

"Awkward," Sky said quietly.

Maggie glanced back over at Boudreaux one more time as they made their way to the Cherokee. He was still watching her.

She was tempted to walk over there and say something, felt as though she should. She hadn't seen or spoken to Boudreaux since the shooting. But what could she say? *I'm sorry I killed your stepson.* It would be a lie. He'd had her ex-husband killed. He'd shot Wyatt. He was going to kill her. She wasn't truly sorry, and Boudreaux knew her well enough to see through the nicety.

What she was sorry for was his pain, and the fact that their odd relationship was no doubt over, but that was probably for the best. She wasn't sure she would have ended their strange, budding friendship on her own.

⚓ ⚓ ⚓

Sheriff Wyatt Hamilton thumped somewhat awkwardly down the hallway at Weems Memorial Hospital. At six-four, he was uncomfortable hunching over the aluminum walker, which seemed like it was built for a geriatric dwarf. Unfortunately, despite the fact that he'd gotten fairly good at using his cane, hospital regulations decreed that it was either the walker or a wheelchair. He supposed they were afraid he'd face-plant in their hallway and sue.

It had been almost a month since he'd been shot by Patrick Boudreaux. He'd cursed the smarmy cokehead through two surgeries, one on his lower intestine, one on his left hip, and through two weeks spent going bat-crap crazy in a hospital bed.

He'd been released almost two weeks ago, but had come to the hospital for one more scan of his hip before heading to Orlando for another surgery, this time with an orthopedic surgeon who was considered one of the best in the state.

Apparently, everything looked as it should, and he'd been given the green light to go ahead with the surgery that just might allow him to get by without the cane, and with perhaps just a slight limp to show for his experience.

Now, he had a few minutes before Maggie would be there to pick him back up, and he was headed over to the lobby to grab a Mountain Dew out of the machine.

He rounded the corner into a wide vestibule off the lobby, where there were four elevators, some restrooms, and two vending machines that promised him happiness and sanity for a dollar a pop. As he thumped his way toward them, the ladies' room door opened, and another aluminum walker thumped through it. The heavy swinging door started to close on the walker, and Wyatt reached out and grabbed it before it could crush the tiny old woman in its path.

She looked up at Wyatt, looked a great distance up, as she couldn't have been more than four foot ten. She was mulatto, maybe Caribbean, and looked to be about a hundred and fifty years old, but her eyes were sharp and huge behind lenses as thick as his pinky finger.

"Thank you," she said, in a voice that reminded Wyatt of sandpaper on wood.

"You're welcome," he said, and let the door close once she'd cleared it.

She looked him up and down, and he suddenly felt like he should have worn something more businesslike to the hospital, instead of cargo shorts and a Hawaiian shirt. He smiled politely and waited for her to proceed, but she just stood there, so they faced each other, walker to walker. He tried not to loom over her, but he felt like a Sandhill crane staring down a baby flamingo.

Finally, she moved aside, her walker gliding smoothly on the tile, and he began thumping past her toward the vending machine. When he got there, he looked over to find her still standing there watching him.

"You need get you some tenny ball f'your walkie talkie," she said to him. "Make for go better."

It took Wyatt a moment to translate that in his head, and he looked down at his walker. "Oh, well, it's the hospital's," he said.

He dug out his wallet and pulled out a dollar bill. As he stuck his wallet back into his pocket, she spoke again.

"Why a big strong young man usin' that thing?"

"Oh. Uh, I got shot," he said. He slid the bill into the slot.

"Who shoot you?" she asked, as though she were planning to give somebody a good talking to.

"A bad guy," he said simply, sliding his bill in a second and third time.

"Why he shoot you?"

"I'm the Sheriff," Wyatt answered, as though that by itself was a reason.

The bill finally went in, and Wyatt almost wept with relief as he punched the correct button and heard the plastic bottle thunk down into the bin. He reached down and grabbed it, and when he straightened up he saw her staring at him, a frown creasing her forehead. He looked down at his clothing, then back up at the old woman.

"No, really," he said.

The old woman looked at him a moment longer. "Juju got that one."

"Juju?"

"Done him in."

He was about to ask her what she meant when a tall woman of about fifty stepped up behind the old lady. Her skin was just a shade darker than the older woman's, but she had the same high cheekbones. Wyatt knew her from somewhere, but couldn't place her.

"Mama, you went the restroom yet?" she asked.

"I went," the old lady said, craning her neck to look up at the younger woman.

"Come on, then," the younger woman said. She looked at Wyatt blankly as she helped her mother turn around and head toward the lobby.

Wyatt looked after them a moment, then focused on unscrewing the cap to his soda and taking a long pull. Then he sat down on a padded bench in the lobby to wait for Maggie and hopefully drink most of his Mountain Dew before she could whine at him about drinking antifreeze. He didn't end up with that much time.

"Hey."

He looked up to see Maggie and Sky approaching.

"Hey," he said.

"Hey, Festus," Sky said with a slight grin.

Wyatt threw her a look. "You remind me so much of your mother," he said. "You're both adorable when you're not talking."

"So how'd it go?" Maggie asked.

"It went fine," Wyatt answered. "I'm good to go."

He stood up, then faltered for a moment as he tried to figure out what to do with his soda. He handed it to Sky. "Here, hold this for me."

"Mom says this stuff has flame retardant in it," Sky said.

"I know," Wyatt said as he started moving along on his walker. "It's part of my safety regimen."

They stopped at the receptionist's desk, and Wyatt grabbed his cane from where it hung on the walker, and turned the walker back in. Then they headed for the front door.

"I just met a Martian, by the way," he said to Maggie.

⚓ ⚓ ⚓

They got to the air taxi hangar at Apalachicola Regional Airport with a good twenty minutes to spare. Wyatt checked in and gave them his overnight bag, then he and Maggie and Sky sat down on the front porch of the "terminal," which looked like a beach cottage more than anything else. Wyatt's plane, a six-seater, was running on the tarmac while the pilot and co-pilot went through their preflight checks.

"Dude, you sure you want to get in that thing?" Sky asked, jerking her head toward the plane. She was holding her phone, one earplug in her ear, leaving the other dangling on her shoulder in an effort to be polite.

"What?" he asked defensively. "It flies."

"Yeah, but does it *keep* flying?"

"It'll get me to Orlando," he said. "Smarty."

He opened his Mountain Dew and finished it off, then tossed it in a waste can beside him.

"I feel bad that you're going to be by yourself until Thursday," Maggie said. Today's flight was the only one the charter company had available this week, and Wyatt was supposed to meet with the surgeon and anesthesiologist early tomorrow morning. His surgery was scheduled for 7am on Thursday.

"Well, quit it," he said. "I'm going to spend lots of quality time with myself at the hotel, eating things that are bad for me and watching ESPN."

"Well, Mom and Dad and the kids are gonna spend the day at Aquatica Thursday, while I wait for you," Maggie said.

"You should go to Aquatica, too," Wyatt. "They said I'll be in surgery for at least four hours, and I'll be out of it for a while after that."

"I prefer to wait," Maggie said.

"Okay, good," he replied. "I prefer it, too. But I had to be polite."

Maggie smiled at him and he gave her one of his winks.

The young, blond man who served as the flight attendant came out of the office, trailed by a middle-aged couple in matching red polo shirts. "We're all set, Sheriff," he said, as he led the couple down the steps.

Wyatt leaned on his cane and stood, and Maggie and Sky stood up as well.

"I'm gonna go wait in the Jeep so you guys can do your thing," Sky said. She stepped over and gave Wyatt a one-armed hug. "See you, Lurch."

"See you later, Wednesday," he answered.

They watched her jump down the steps and head to the Jeep, tucking her other earplug back in on the way. Then Wyatt turned back to Maggie.

"Well. I guess I'll see you in a couple days," he said.

Maggie leaned over to kiss him, and he started to bend down, then put a hand on her shoulder to stop her. "Hold on," he said.

He went down the steps, then held out a hand to her. She took it, and he pulled her down to the next to last step so that they were eye to eye.

"There we go. Leaning's still not my best thing," he said. He ducked his head and kissed her, slow and sweet and tasting faintly of mint and Mountain Dew. "I'll see you Thursday," he said when he lifted his head. "It's the Quality Suites next to the hospital. They've got your rooms reserved."

"Maybe when you wake up we can watch a movie in your room and share your morphine drip," Maggie said. "We can call it our second date."

"Crap no," he said. "No more second dates. Let's skip the second date and go for a third date instead."

The first time they'd tried to have a second date, Maggie had been shot. The second time, Wyatt had been shot. "That sounds like a good plan," Maggie said. "I'm tired of waiting for an asteroid to hit me."

She stepped down to the tarmac and gave Wyatt a hug. "I'll see you."

"See ya," he said, and started toward the plane. Halfway there, he stopped and turned around. "I think I look pretty cool with a cane, don't you? Kind of dapper, like a retired secret agent or something."

Maggie grinned at him. "Yep, dapper's the word I was searching for."

He waggled his eyebrows at her, then turned and headed for his plane.

CHAPTER
THREE

luff Road ran northwest from town for about five miles, before it abruptly dead-ended. Just before the dead end, a dirt road led onto Maggie's five acres on the river. Maggie turned off onto the gravel, and they bumped along through woods for a quarter mile before reaching the cypress stilt house that her father's father had built.

The back of the property curved outward into the river, and was bound on the northwest side by the respectably-sized Cypress Creek, so that there was water both alongside the house on the northwest side, and, several hundred yards back in the woods, also on the northeast. It meant they almost always had a decent breeze, and Maggie was pretty sure Grandpa had positioned the house the way he had to take advantage of that. A wraparound deck made the most of it.

The dirt drive ended in a mostly-gravel circle out front that they used for parking, and Maggie pulled the Jeep in next to the old Toyota pick-up that had belonged to Sky's father, and now belonged to Sky.

Before Maggie had turned off the engine, their Catahoula Parish Leopard Hound, Coco, came barreling out from behind the house somewhere. She threw herself into the grass at Maggie's feet and commenced writhing in joyful agony, despite the fact that they'd only been gone a few hours.

As Maggie squatted down to rub Coco's belly, the sounds of an elderly man having a coughing fit came from across the yard. She looked up to see her Ameraucana rooster flailing toward her at his typical breakneck pace, wings and neck feathers extended to their fullest and most impressive potential.

In his oddly broken crow, he advised her with his usual urgency that she had returned, or that all was well, or that all was not. His reports tended to be vague, but vital.

"Thank you, Stoopid," Maggie said as she stood up, and then whistled sharply at Coco as the dog chased Stoopid for a few steps. Coco and Stoopid were roughly the same age, and had grown up together more or less, but it amused them to torment each other on occasion.

Coco halted, and Stoopid ran a few more feet, then turned and showed Coco how menacing he looked with wings akimbo, before stalking off in obvious triumph.

"I swear, our animals are like other people's crazy relatives," Sky said as they headed for the stairs to the deck.

"Yeah, but they suit us," Maggie answered as they climbed the stairs. The third step from the top sagged and swayed a bit, reminding Maggie that she and Daddy needed to finally replace the support pole beneath it, or have a professional come do it. She made a mental note to take care of it when they got back from Orlando.

After letting Coco in and dumping her purse on the dining room table that sat just inside the front door, Maggie started packing suitcases for herself and the kids. Her ten-year-old son, Kyle, had gone on a camping trip in Tate's Hell State Forest with his friend Brian and his family, and would be back around dinnertime. She planned to get them all to bed early, and head out around five in the morning.

Around noon, Maggie's cell phone rang, and she saw that it was Brian's father, Jason.

"Hey, Jason," Maggie answered.

"Hey, Maggie. Listen, we're going to head on back to town," Jason said. "I hear on the radio that Faye's been upgraded to a Cat 1, and she's beating the crap out of Naples right now."

"Yeah, I was watching the Weather Channel earlier," Maggie said. "But they said she was headed northwest, back out into the Gulf."

"Well, now they're thinking she might just keep moving straight up the coast," Jason said. "She hasn't veered off yet."

Maggie sighed, as thirty-seven things added themselves to her to-do list. "Okay, thanks, Jason. Are you coming back now?"

"Yeah, we're breaking camp right now. We should be dropping him off in an hour or so. You home?"

"Yeah, I'll be here. I think I'll board up, then we'll go ahead and leave tonight."

"You still need us to come by and feed the dog and the chickens while you're gone?"

"No, I'll take Coco with me," Maggie said. She'd take the chickens, too, if she could. "The chickens are going to be put up in the concrete shed, and I'll make sure they have enough food and water to last."

"Okay then. We'll see you in a bit," Jason said, and hung up.

Maggie sighed again, and headed down the hall to Sky's room, Coco on her heels, the dog's toenails tapping against the hardwood floor.

Maggie stopped in Sky's open doorway. Sky was packing. Tinny, obnoxious music leaked from her earbuds. She looked up and spotted Maggie, pulled one earbud out.

"We're gonna have to go ahead and get ready for a storm," Maggie said. "Faye might move up the coast."

"What about Coco?"

"She's coming with us."

"Do they allow dogs at the hotel?"

"They will," Maggie said. "Let's get the windows boarded up, then we're going to need to move Stoopid and The Girls over to the shed. Kyle will be home in about an hour to help."

"Chicken herding. This is gonna be awesome," Sky said with an eye-roll.

"Yeah, all kinds of fun," Maggie agreed, and she and Coco headed back up the hall.

⚓ ⚓ ⚓

Maggie and Sky were almost halfway through boarding up the windows when Kyle got home. Jason had offered to stay and help, but Maggie knew he needed to make preparations at his own home, and she and the kids had gotten pretty good at it over the years. Maggie held the sheets of plywood up and Sky drilled them in. With Kyle to help hold them up from the bottom, the rest of the job went more quickly.

Moving The Girls from the chicken yard to the concrete shed went less smoothly. The shed was a small, concrete block affair, which sat on a foundation of even more concrete blocks, that her grandfather had put up to store tools and parts for his oyster skiff. Those had been gone for years, though the skiff itself was still moored to the dock behind the house.

A few years back, Maggie had cleared out the shed and added some perches for the chickens, in preparation for a tropical storm that had gone fickle and decided not to show up. She had Kyle throw some straw down and fill the automatic waterer and the food and grit pans. She and Sky commenced herding the dozen hens from the chicken pen to the shed twenty feet away. It was a lot like chasing clowns from one clown car into another. Stoopid actually helped out somewhat, chasing Miss Mathilda around in circles until she wore out and allowed herself to be yanked up and carried.

Stoopid himself wasn't that easy. The three of them chased him around the yard until he finally flapped up onto a tree limb just out of reach. Maggie tried coaxing him with feed, lettuce, and finally Cheetos, to no avail. She eventually threw up her hands, tossed him a few choice words, and vowed to catch him later.

By six o'clock, the wind had picked up considerably, the sky had grown steely gray, and the Weather Channel was reporting that Hurricane Faye was still a Cat 1, but had stalled just west of Cedar Key and was picking up a great deal of water to add to the already torrential rains. Panhandle residents were being advised to prepare their homes and move inland.

Maggie and the kids had loaded up the Jeep and were grabbing a few last items when Maggie dialed Wyatt on her cell.

"Hey," he answered. "What's going on with your weather?"

"Things are starting to get windy," she said. "No rain yet, though. Kyle came home early, so we're getting ready to head out now."

Maggie turned around and looked at Coco, who was growling and pacing in front of the door. She'd been agitated for several minutes. She hated storms, and the wind had started rattling the porch furniture and flower pots and other miscellaneous things outside. Maggie slapped her thigh to call Coco, but was ignored.

"How long's it going to take you to get to Jax?" Wyatt was asking.

"Well, I'm thinking quite a few people are heading inland, so traffic might suck a little. We should be there around eleven or so, though."

"I'll probably be asleep by then," Wyatt said. "I have to be at the hospital at seven-thirty. But call me if you need to."

Coco let out a low bark at the front window. "Coco, it's fine," Maggie said, then turned her attention back to the call. "I will. I've gotta run. I need to charge my phone and catch Stoopid."

"Is he coming to Orlando, too?"

"Maybe in a crock pot," Maggie said. "Get some rest and I'll call you in the morning."

"Okee-doke. Be careful."

Maggie hung up and went to the window by the front door, where Coco stood growling. When she looked out to the yard, Maggie's heart flipped a bit. Stoopid was in the middle of the gravel parking area, flapping and crowing, leaning into the wind. Coco barked sharply, and Maggie took her collar, led her back to her bedroom, and closed the door. She didn't need Coco outside, too.

As Maggie opened the front door, Stoopid started toward the house, then a gust dumped him onto his butt. He righted himself, only to get blown a few feet through the gravel. Maggie ran down the stairs.

The winds had picked up considerably, and Maggie judged them to be a good 20mph. She hopped over a terra cotta flower pot as it rolled toward her feet, and ran after her rooster, who was rolling into the grass.

Apparently, he wasn't panicked enough to be sure he wanted rescue, because he flailed away from her when she reached down to pick him up. She cursed him, as she heard Kyle call into the wind from the deck.

"Mom?" he called, his voice uncertain.

"It's okay," she yelled over her shoulder. "I'll get him."

She ran a few steps, then had to pivot as Stoopid got blown to the side.

"Mom?" Kyle called again, sounding worried.

"Kyle, it's okay! Wait inside."

She made one last leap at Stoopid as he flapped on his back, and scooped him up with a grunt. "Peck me and I'll punch you right in the face," she growled.

She didn't want to risk opening the shed door and having one or more of the hens make a dash for it. She was going to have to set Stoopid up in the house and deal with the chicken poop when she got back. She turned around to head for the house, and felt as though all of her internal organs had stopped functioning at once.

Kyle stood at the top of the stairs. The man from the flower shop stood behind him, one hand on the neck of her little boy, the other holding a gun to his temple.

CHAPTER FOUR

As Maggie stood there, Stoopid still in her grip, the sound of blood rushing in her ears overtook the sounds of the wind. Her eyes were locked on Kyle's. His sleek, black hair whipped across his eyes, but she could still see them, bright green, large and frightened. For a moment, his fear, and the gun at his temple, were the only things that existed for Maggie. And then she wondered, *Where's Sky?* She felt ice forming in her chest, could feel it sealing and cracking over her lungs and her heart. She had known terror before, but her children had never been in danger. This was a level of fear beyond her experience.

"Get up here, real nice and slow," the man said over the wind.

Maggie started for the stairs, and she was vaguely aware of being surprised that Stoopid hadn't moved a muscle, though his little heart was pounding beneath her hand. As she walked up the stairs, her eyes flicked back and forth between Kyle's and the man's. The man's eyes were cold, yet agitated, maybe even a little frightened, but his gun hand didn't tremble.

The gun was a .22, and things broke inside of Maggie as she remembered everything she knew about gunshots to the head with a 22-caliber. The way the small rounds tended to bounce around inside the skull, inflicting horrific brain damage, even if they didn't kill. She swallowed hard and ascended the stairs.

When she got to the shaky step, the stair and the piling beneath it wobbled a bit, but she expected it, and her eyes remained locked onto the man's, as he backed up the few steps into the house, looking over his shoulder quickly before he moved inside.

Maggie followed him into the dining area just inside the door. She could hear Coco barking and growling from behind her closed bedroom door, but her attention was immediately drawn away from Coco to Sky, who was lying on the floor of the small, open kitchen, unconscious or worse.

The man saw where she was looking. "She ain't dead. But she can be, if you try to get cute with me. Get rid of that roo and close the door."

Maggie knew he meant for her to dump Stoopid outside, but instead she tossed him onto the dining room table, then reached back and shut the door. The man looked at her like she was an idiot, but he didn't say anything. Stoopid flapped around on the table with a confused cough, then jumped down to the floor and high-stepped into the living area.

Maggie took a deep breath. "What do you want?" she asked, sounding far calmer than she was.

"What do I want?" the man repeated, his eyes narrow and full of hate. He held onto Kyle's shoulder as they moved slowly toward her. The barrel of the gun never left Kyle's skin. "So far I've got what I want."

"My son?" Maggie asked, blinking rapidly.

The man stopped just inches from her. "Your *son!*" he said, with something close to disgust in his voice, and he raised his hand off of Kyle's shoulder. She caught Kyle's eye for a split second, terrified he would instinctively try to move away because the hand was gone. Then the upper cut slammed into her chin before her brain could tell her to block it.

⚓ ⚓ ⚓

When Maggie came around, she was lying on the wood floor, her hands tied tightly behind her back. She could hear Coco, still barking from her bedroom. Before she blinked her eyes open, she fully expected Kyle to be gone. He wasn't.

Kyle and Sky were sitting next to each other on the far side of the dining room table. Maggie's throat tightened with gratitude that Sky was conscious. There was a reddened mound on her left temple where a serious bruise would soon appear, but she seemed otherwise unharmed. Her arms were tied together around the back of the chair, and the man from the flower shop was bent behind Kyle, apparently tying his as well.

Maggie sat up with a grunt. It took some effort, and was awkward because of the ropes that bound her wrists. The man glanced over at her, then back to his work. The eyes of both of her children locked onto hers.

The fear in those eyes, and the damage to Sky's face, brought a slow, warm wave of anger to Maggie, one that she welcomed. Anger had rescued her from fear more than once. Fear for her children had been almost paralyzing, but rage calmed her. She could think clearly through it. This man was at a serious advantage. He was armed and she was unable to get to her weapons at the moment. The only way she would be able to save her kids was by thinking clearly.

Maggie scooted back on her butt until she hit the wall, then slumped against it. She stared back at her beautiful little boy, who was wincing as his wrists were tied.

"It's okay, Kyle," she said softly. "It'll be okay."

The man looked at her over Kyle's shoulder. "That's not for you to say, is it?" He finished up with Kyle and slowly walked around the table toward Maggie. He stopped a couple of feet away and stared down at her. "I decide what's gonna be okay."

"What do you want?" Maggie asked again, trying not to sound too combative.

"I'll let you wonder about that for a while," he said quietly. "Where's your gun?"

Maggie didn't answer. He only waited for a few seconds before swinging his gun arm around and aiming at Kyle. "I don't care about your kids," he said. "I really don't care about your kids. So, you either tell me where it is or you'll have one less kid. If I have to go find it myself, you won't have any kids at all."

Maggie tabulated possible answers and their outcomes. He might not want to go into her room because of Coco. Or, he might go in there to shut Coco up, and then he'd see her Glock sitting on her bed next to her overnight bag. He already had a gun. She had no way to use hers at the moment. It really didn't change anything for him to have her weapon, too, but lying to him might change a lot of things.

"It's in my bedroom. On my bed."

"Which one's your bedroom?"

"The noisy one."

"Looks like we have a problem," the man said. "I want that gun, but I'd sooner kill a human being than kill a decent dog."

Maggie's heart lurched. "Please don't hurt her," she said quietly.

"If she comes at me, I'll kill her."

"She won't, if I tell her it's okay."

"She gonna believe that?"

"No. But she'll listen anyway."

The man reached down and grabbed her by the hair. "Get up."

Maggie struggled to her feet clumsily. He helped by lifting her up by her ponytail.

"We're gonna go get that gun. You're gonna control that dog." He jerked the gun toward the table. "Go stand over there."

Maggie walked over to the table and stood at the close end, the place where her late ex-husband David sat for dinner. No one sat there for dinner now, unless her parents were over. Kyle and Sky both looked up at her, and she hoped her face was reassuring.

"Over there, by the couch," the man said. "Outa my way."

Maggie moved a few feet toward the hallway, stopped and turned around at the end of the couch. The man stepped behind Kyle's chair. Maggie noted that Kyle's wrists were bound with a handcuff knot. Not one she would have chosen, but she noted that the man had used a length of rope she'd had hanging out on the deck. There'd only been a few yards. Maybe he'd chosen the knot because it didn't require much rope. That would also explain why he hadn't tied their wrists to the chairs. She would have.

The man lifted Kyle up by one underarm. "Come on, boy."

"What are you doing?" Maggie asked.

The man grinned at her. It wasn't a pleasant grin. "I ain't stupid. I think you'd be willing to let your dog at me, even if I did shoot her. Might buy you enough time to grab your gun, wouldn't it?"

He put the barrel of his gun back to Kyle's temple, and jerked his chin at Maggie. "Let's go. You get that dog there to calm down, and you don't go in that room, hear me?"

Maggie turned and started walking down the hallway. Coco must have smelled her, because she stopped barking and whined. "Coco, it's okay, baby. Hush." Coco whined back, then was quiet.

Maggie stopped at the closed door and turned around. The man and Kyle were six feet or so behind her.

"How am I supposed to open the door?" she asked quietly.

"You'll figure it out."

Maggie backed up to the door and tried to lift her arms enough to reach the doorknob, but she couldn't. She stood up on her tippy toes, and after several slaps at the knob she heard the catch come open.

"Watch yourself," the man said, and Maggie couldn't help but look at the gun barrel on the side of her little boy's head. Kyle's eyes were impossibly wide, and his knees were shaking visibly.

"Coco, sit!" Maggie commanded. "Stay."

The man moved Kyle forward as Maggie let the door swing slowly inward. He and Kyle were no more than three feet behind her.

Coco was sitting near the foot of the bed, pointing her face toward Maggie and trying hard not to stand up, but her butt was lifted off of the floor a couple of inches before Maggie spoke. "Coco, sit!" she said sharply.

She looked over her shoulder at the man.

"You walk in there, real slow like. Get over there by her."

Maggie backed up slowly until she was standing next to her dog. Coco let out a low growl, then nudged at Maggie's leg. "Shh, quiet. It's okay."

The man looked over Kyle's shoulder from the doorway, spotted Maggie's service weapon on the bed. He stared at Coco for a moment, then, his hand still under Kyle's arm, guided the boy over to the bed. When they got there, he pressed the gun barrel harder against Kyle's temple.

"Don't you move, boy," he said, then let go of Kyle's arm, and bent just enough to snatch up the Glock in its holster. He shoved it into the front waistband of his jeans, then grabbed Kyle's arm again.

"You got any more guns in here?"

"No."

"Don't lie to me. You got a gun in that closet?"

"No. I don't."

He yanked Kyle with him as he stepped over to the nightstand and opened the small drawer. There was nothing in there but a couple of paperbacks and some hair clips. He shut the drawer, then pointed at the small, open closet behind Maggie. "Let me see in there."

Maggie walked over to the closet. She toed the door all the way open, and he looked at the floor, and on the shelf above the clothes, where several plastic shoe boxes were stacked.

"Let's go," the man said to Maggie. "Us first, then you. The dog stays in here."

Maggie waited and watched as the man and Kyle edged back out into the hallway. Kyle was small for his age, but he had never looked smaller. The man stopped and jerked his chin at Maggie. "Come on," he said.

"Stay, Coco," Maggie said, and she walked to the doorway. "The door," she said to the man.

"Come over here," he answered. She moved a few feet
down the hallway, and the man edged back over to the
door. Coco watched him, but didn't growl and didn't stand.
He let go of Kyle long enough to pull the door shut, then
jerked his chin toward the living room. "Go on."

Maggie turned back around, and saw Stoopid at the
end of the hall, watching them. When they started walking back, the rooster turned and trotted back out the living room.

"Sit down over there," the man said, pointing his chin
at David's chair. Maggie walked over and sat down, meeting Sky's gaze as she did.

The man sat Kyle back down in the chair and looked at
Maggie.

"A cop, a *woman* who likes to shoot things, livin' way
out here, she's got more than a .45 layin' around. Where's
the rest of your guns?"

Maggie rapidly tried to calculate, again, the possible
outcomes of dishonesty.

"Don't think so hard," the man said. "I'll look, and I'll
find 'em. When I do, I'll use one of *them* on him." He put
the gun against the back of Kyle's head, then swung it over
to point at Sky. "Or her."

Maggie knew he would find them. Her weapons were
situated more for easy access than for concealment. She
wasn't sure he would shoot one of her kids if she lied to
him, but she wasn't sure he wouldn't, either. He already
had enough firepower to kill all three of them. Allowing
him to collect her guns wasn't going to worsen their situation. If anything, maybe he'd actually help her by consoli-
dating them for her.

"There's a shotgun on the top shelf of the hall closet," she said. She paused and let out a slow breath. "And a .38 on top of the fridge."

The man smiled just a bit, and walked over the fridge, which was at the edge of the open kitchen. She watched him easily reach up and pat around until he found the revolver that had belonged to her grandfather. As he pulled the gun out, he knocked against the old tin that held the extra rounds. He tucked the revolver in the back of his jeans and pulled out the tin, shaking it.

Sky looked at Maggie, and Maggie could tell that she disagreed with Maggie's choice to be straightforward. Maggie let out a breath and watched as the man stepped over to the hall closet, poked around, and then pulled the Mossberg out from behind the stacks of towels.

"Nice," he said. "I might keep this."

CHAPTER

FIVE

T he three of them watched as the man walked into the kitchen and dumped the shotgun and two handguns onto the kitchen counter. Then he set his own gun down and unloaded Maggie's weapons.

As Maggie watched him, she tried to assess him, and their situation, a bit better. He'd been in the flower shop and heard them talk about leaving town. If he'd been interested in robbing them, he wouldn't be here yet. He wanted something from her, or he wanted to do something to her. Maggie's guess was that he already knew who she was when he'd seen her there that morning, maybe even followed her there. But he seemed disorganized, unprepared, as though coming here today had been an improvisation. Because they were leaving town?

The man finished removing the shells from the Mossberg, dumped them on the counter, then glanced over at her cell phone, which was charging on the counter. He reached over and pulled it off the charger, held it up as he looked over at them.

"Where's the rest of 'em?" He looked at Sky. "Where's your phone?"

Sky glared at him, then cleared her throat. "My back pocket."

He stalked over to her. "Get up." Sky struggled to her feet, and he yanked the phone, still hooked up to her earbuds, out of the pocket of her jeans. Then he looked at Kyle. "Where's yours, boy?"

Kyle stared up at the man, his eyes wide. "Speak, boy!" the man barked, and Maggie wanted him dead.

"It's in my backpack. Over there," Kyle said in a small voice, jerking his head back toward the living room.

The man stalked over to the living room and started rifling through Kyle's backpack on the window seat. He pulled out Kyle's phone, then went back into the kitchen and dropped the phones on the counter. Then he came back to the dining area and started panning around the room, and looked at Maggie.

"Where's the keys for those vehicles out there?"

Maggie felt her heart skip a couple of beats at the hope that he was going to steal her Jeep and leave, even though she knew that wasn't very logical. Nobody kidnapped a cop and two children to steal a ten-year-old Cherokee.

"They're right there, on the hook," Maggie said, looking over toward the front door. The keys for both trucks, extra keys for her Daddy's boats, and a few that had forgotten uses hung in a row on the wall.

He walked over to the set of hooks by the front door, reached up. "Which ones?"

"The Seafood Festival keychain. Those are mine," Maggie said.

The man yanked them off the peg and looked over his shoulder at her. "What about the pickup?"

"That's my Dad's truck!" Sky snapped.

He glared over at her. "I don't care whose it is, girl. Where's the keys?"

"The set with the little Rubik's cube," Maggie said. Sky looked at Maggie desperately. "It's okay. Granddad has a spare."

"But that's Daddy's Rubik's cube," Sky said.

"Where's your Daddy at, girl?" the man asked as he yanked down the keys.

"He's dead," Sky said defiantly, raising her chin.

"Too bad," he said, in a tone that indicated it wasn't. He moved back to the hall closet and yanked out the gym bag that Maggie kept on the floor, carried it into the kitchen. Maggie and the kids watched as he unzipped it, tossed in the revolver and tin of ammo, the Glock, and finally the Mossberg, then zipped everything back up.

Maggie saw the look of hope on both her children's faces, and she wished that she could hope with them, then pitied them for it.

He picked up the cell phones and keys and looked like he was going to drop them in, too, then he looked around a moment before stalking out the front door. He left the door open and Maggie's and the kids' heads followed the sound of his boots as he walked across the front deck to the creek side. A moment later, he came back in empty-handed.

"What'd you do that for?" Sky snapped.

"You don't need 'em," he answered, then looked at Maggie.

"Let's go," he said.

They were words that Maggie didn't really expect, but they didn't shock her, either. She glanced over at the kids as she stood up. If anything, Kyle looked even more frightened than he already had.

"Mom?" he asked, his voice cracking.

Sky started to get to her feet, and the man swung the .22 in her direction. "Not you. Sit down."

"Where are you taking her?" Sky demanded, and while Maggie was proud of her bravery, she wanted her to shut up.

"Shut up and sit back down," the man said, then grabbed Maggie under one arm and jerked her up.

One of the many things she had had drilled into her head in her training, and had since drilled into her children's heads, was to never allow someone to take her to another location. Wherever someone wanted to take you, it was more private, it was safer for them somehow, and it was the future location of your death.

In this case, though, allowing herself to be taken out of the house meant getting this man away from her children, and that was a game-changer for which she would gladly break the rule.

The man shoved her toward the front door, and Maggie turned around and looked at her children, who were staring back at her. She felt herself trying to memorize them, even as she tried to look reassuring. Then the man opened the door and shoved her back around.

"Move it," he said. Maggie walked out onto the deck, as a first crack of thunder rolled through the air in the distance. The sky had grown darker in the short time they'd been inside. How long?

Maggie had just taken a step toward the stairs when two shots rang out behind her. She spun, hoping she would be dead before she looked back inside the house.

The man was standing there in the doorway, the gun pointed at the sky, and he was smiling. "Gotcha, didn't I?" he said, and Maggie knew that if she had even the smallest opportunity, she would kill him, and badly.

⚓ ⚓ ⚓

Once they were down the deck stairs, the man directed Maggie to walk up the dirt drive. He followed closely behind her. To the west, the sky seemed to grow a deeper shade of gray every moment. The wind was erratic; it seemed to have slowed a bit, but occasional gusts whipped at Maggie's T-shirt and the strands of hair that had fallen or been pulled loose from her ponytail.

Maggie couldn't help feeling like she was being marched out in front of a firing squad, and she was distractedly surprised that thoughts of how, where, and when this man was going to kill her weren't really uppermost in her mind. Instead, her mind seemed to skip around between thoughts of how Kyle's hair smelled after his shower, the way Wyatt's dimples deepened when he gave her one of his silly grins, or the image of Sky rolling her eyes, earbud wires hanging from her ears.

It wasn't so much that her life was flashing before her eyes, as it was an involuntary inventory of the small things that made her life seem bigger than it was. She sensed, though, that allowing her mind to roam freely among these artifacts would also allow her feelings to overwhelm and weaken her, so she forced herself to focus on the sound of her boots on the dirt road, the smell of cold metal in the storm's humidity, and the way her wrists were beginning to numb and burn almost simultaneously. When she had cleared her head, she tried to think.

Once they were removed from the kids, her options were going to change. Her chances of survival were going to get smaller, but her willingness to take risks would be much greater. The truth was, her chances of survival were nonexistent. Any move, regardless of its chances of success,

would improve her likelihood of making it through whatever this creep had planned.

She hadn't had much time yet to try to peg this man
who had burst into her life and completely changed her re-
ality. Now that she knew for sure that she was his objec-
tive, she was pretty sure he'd known she was in the flower shop before he'd walked in. So, this wasn't a random
thing, or an impulse. Maybe the timing was impulsive, but
not the targeting.

He seemed self-confident, but the confidence was in
himself, not in some plan. She didn't think he actually had
one. He seemed to make moves and decisions as he went.
No, he had targeted her at some point, but his decision to
come here today, in this way, was an impulsive one.

He hated her. Either that, or just hated in general. Making her think he'd shot her kids was cruel. He liked hurting her, whether that was because he liked hurting people
in general, or because he had it in for her, she wasn't sure.
What she was sure of was that she didn't know him.

She was half expecting someone to be waiting down her
road with a running vehicle. But instead, when she rounded a bend, she saw a late 70s model Chevy pickup parked
alongside the drainage ditch, facing her house. She stopped
and turned around to face the man.

"Go on," he said roughly, pointing his gun arm in the
direction of the truck.

Maggie turned back around, and the man grabbed her
under the arm and propelled her the rest of the way to the
truck. She heard her weapons tapping against each other
in the gym bag on his shoulder, and would have given one
of her legs to be pointing one of them, any of them, at the
man's face.

When they were a couple of feet from the truck, he gave her a shove, and she landed against the truck bed. The driver's side door issued a metallic groan as he pulled it open.

"Get in and get over," he said, pointing the .22 at her.

Maggie bit the inside of her cheek as she ran through her options at the speed of thought. There weren't any good ones.

She turned and tried to get up on the running board, but couldn't do it without grabbing onto something. He made a disgusted noise and grabbed her underarm again and hoisted her.

She fell onto the bench seat and scooted over and up against the passenger door. She watched him toss the gym bag into the truck bed, then he got in, still training the gun on her. He wasn't aiming anywhere in particular, but he'd have to try pretty hard to miss her.

The keys were in the ignition, and after he shut his door, he switched the gun to his left hand and turned the key. Nothing. Not even a click. He did it again, and then a third time, then slammed his palm against the steering wheel hard enough to rock the truck. He cursed, then slammed it again and again until he seemed to have gotten it out of his system, but when he turned to look at her, she could see rage and a little bit of panic on his face. She wondered if he could see the loss of hope on hers.

"Now what?" she asked.

"Shut up!" he yelled. "Shut the hell up!"

Maggie took a breath and waited, watched him as he glared out the windshield for a moment. Then he switched the gun back to his right hand and jerked open his door.

"Let's go," he said.

He got out and waited as she looked at him for a moment, wondering if he would just walk back to town if she made him shoot her right there in the truck, but the chances of that were slim. It was almost five miles, and a storm was coming. Her house was just a few hundred yards up the road.

She slid across the seat to the other door, and he pulled her out of the truck. She stumbled a bit before she got her footing, then watched him grab the gym bag out of the back and jerk it back onto his shoulder.

"Go on," he said.

She heard him slam the door behind her as she started walking slowly back up the road. She felt a lurch in her chest as she realized that she would see her kids again. It was quickly replaced by guilt for thinking it, and a determination that this man might get back into her house, but she wouldn't be escorting him there.

If she took a chance and blew it, she would be dead and he would be alone with her kids. In all likelihood, he wouldn't leave them alive a second time. But if she let him parade her back to the house, their chances weren't much better.

If she could put him out of commission somehow, or at least beat him back to the house, their odds of survival improved just a bit. At least they would have odds. She thought about just taking off into the woods, which she knew like the back of her hand, but he wouldn't follow. He knew enough to know that all he had to do was return to the house and she would walk right back to him.

As Maggie tried to come up with a viable idea, the wind started rifling through the leaves, sounding like thousands of office workers shuffling their paperwork, and she knew the rain was right behind them. They were probably about to start getting squalls from the northern band of Hurricane Faye.

When they were about a hundred yards from the last bend in the drive, Maggie's brain sped up its hunt for an idea that wasn't guaranteed to fail. Once they were past the bend, it was a couple of hundred yards of open clearing all the way to the house. Maggie shuffled through and rejected fractions of ideas, but in the end, it was instinct and opportunity that dictated her move, with no conscious decision to act.

The man shoved her, with a palm between her shoulder blades, and she made more of the stumble than she needed to. She bent forward at the waist like she was about to go down, then slammed her right leg back and upward, straight as a board. She felt it connect with his crotch before she heard his grunt, and she righted herself and spun around.

He hadn't grabbed at himself, but he was halfway to his knees, and she kicked him again in the chin. With her arms behind her back, she had less leverage and power than she would have liked, but it was enough to throw him to his back. She moved in before he could focus, and kicked the gun out of his hand.

It only skittered a few feet on the rough dirt road, but at least it was out of his hand for a moment. She raised her foot again, intending to kick him in the temple, but he was ready, one arm patting the ground beside him for the gun, the other waiting to grab her or block her kick. Rather than hand him her leg, she turned and ran.

She didn't hear his footfalls behind her right away, and she wondered if he was aiming the .22 at her back. She could already feel the heat of the bullet at the base of her spine. But then she did hear him giving chase, and wondered why he *hadn't* shot her.

She had no plan for once she did reach the house. Reaching it first was her only plan. Having her arms behind her made her stride slower and unbalanced, but if she had just a few seconds in her favor, just enough to get the door open and slam the deadbolt home behind her, it would buy them some time. What she would do with it, she wasn't sure, but she prayed the answer would present itself.

His gait sounded uneven behind her, but he was getting nearer. It was hard for her to judge how near. She was running too fast, and making too much noise of her own.

As she came into the front yard area, she felt an expanding in her chest that had nothing to do with the exertion of running. The kids were right there. Right up there behind that door.

She managed to push herself just a bit faster, and had just hit the second stair when the butt of the gun slammed down onto the back of her neck. She seemed to go down and up at the same time somehow, landing almost vertical on the stairs. With no way to break her fall, she had to watch the step rush toward her face, and she slammed nose-first into it.

She instinctively rolled to her side a bit to get off of her face, and blinked a few times against the blinding pain. She could hear him wheezing, felt the stairs shake a bit as he leaned against the rail.

A couple of inches in front of her eyes was a bright red pool as big as her palm. As she watched, two fat raindrops splashed down into it. Then she heard him grunt, and his boot slammed into her side.

W hen the man opened the door, Sky and Kyle stared in shock for a moment. Sky was out of her chair, and was squatting down behind Kyle's with her back to him, trying to get his wrists untied. She hadn't made much headway, if any.

"Mom!" Kyle yelled.

"What did you do?" Sky screamed at the man.

"Get back in that chair," the man snapped. As Sky did as she was told, the man shoved Maggie hard, and she fell to the floor a few feet from the table. She managed to land mostly on her left side, and to protect her face from another slam, but her right side screamed at her and she wondered if he'd broken one of her ribs, or if this was just what it felt like to take a boot to the torso. She didn't know she was going to pass out until she did.

When she came around, she was on her back. Her hands had gone numb, but her wrists hurt from her weight pressing them against the wood floor, and she rolled herself partly onto her left side again. A few inches from her face was an already slightly tacky pool of blood about five inches around. Rooster tracks ran into and out of it in several places.

Maggie curled her body a bit so that she could see the dining room table. The kids' feet were still in front of their chairs. Beyond them, the man's boots paced from the dining room table to the kitchen counter several times. Maggie struggled for a moment, but finally managed to sit up. Her side protested, and she could have sworn she heard something creaking inside of her.

She scooted over and back a bit on her butt, until she could slump back against the back of the couch. The kids watched her over their shoulders, and Maggie tried to give them some kind of reassuring look, but she doubted it had come across that way.

"Are you okay, Mom?" Sky asked. Maggie managed a nod.

"Shut up!" the man barked.

Maggie looked over at him. He'd stopped by the kitchen counter and was pulling a cell phone out of his back pocket. Maggie watched him dial and wait for an answer. Apparently, he didn't get one, because he disconnected the call. He smacked the phone down onto the counter, then slammed his palm down on the countertop.

"What's going on?" Sky asked Maggie, twisting her neck to look on Maggie's direction.

"His truck won't start."

"Y'all shut up," the man said.

Sky turned back around and looked at the table. "Too bad my Dad's keys are in the creek," she said.

"Get in my face and you will be, too," he said, his voice quieter, but menacing.

Sky gave him an insolent look, but then shifted in her seat and stared at a spot on the front door.

For the next hour or so, Maggie and the kids listened to the rain pounding the tin roof, and the wind rattling at the boarded windows. Every now and then, something would scrape or bang up against one of the house's pilings, or into one of the boarded windows. If it had been any other time, Maggie and the kids would have sat around the table, talking about past storms and wondering if the garden would be okay.

They watched the man pace around the house like an outside dog that had been forced to stay inside. He wandered around the living room and kitchen, opening cupboards, turning his head sideways to read the spines of the books that almost filled one wall. He didn't look at Maggie or the kids very often; he almost seemed to avoid it, and that worried Maggie.

He tried placing a call several more times, but never spoke to anyone. He didn't leave a voice mail, either, and Maggie wondered if his cell service was out.

Every now and then, Maggie heard whining coming from underneath her door at the end of the hall, and she knew that Coco had her nose pressed into the crack at the bottom, as she used to do when Maggie was still married, and she and David would close the bedroom door behind them.

The man finally settled down a bit, and leaned up against the counter, drinking a Dr. Pepper he'd pulled out of their fridge.

When Maggie opened her mouth to speak, she had to clear her throat. She could taste blood in the back of her mouth. "Can one of us please give my dog some water?"

"No," he said.

"She left you alone," Maggie said. "It's hot in there with the windows boarded up. Please just let her have some water."

"You thinkin' I'm gonna untie you, or one of them, to give your dog a drink?" He grinned at her like she was stupid.

"Then you do it," Maggie said.

"Let me tell you somethin', lady. You treating me like an idiot isn't gonna help you much."

He drained his Dr. Pepper and, as he lowered it, caught Kyle's eye. His lip curled a bit, and he turned away to toss the empty can in the sink. Then he grabbed a small mixing bowl from the drainer and filled it half full from the tap.

Maggie watched him walk down the hall to her bedroom, and heard Coco's low growl from under the door. The man bent and poured the water under the door, then came back with the empty bowl.

"You happy now, boy?" he asked, and dropped the bowl onto the counter.

"You're a regular Shriner," Sky said.

"Keep runnin' your mouth, girl," he said.

Sky looked away from him, and he resumed his pacing.

CHAPTER
SEVEN

everal hours later, she wasn't sure how many, Maggie
heard Stoopid tap up the hall and into the living room
from one of the kids' rooms. He half-walked, half-
flapped around the room, then located her behind the
couch, and proceeded to advise her, in quiet, almost hen-
like *brrps* that his dinner was late, the weather was inclem-
ent, or that her situation looked grim.

Maggie glanced over at the man, who was sitting at the
far end of the dining room table. He'd been there for some
time, and had either ignored her questions or told her shut
up every time she'd tried to engage him in conversation.

Kyle, and then Sky, had eventually fallen asleep with
their heads on the table. Maggie had nodded off a couple of
times, but only for a few minutes. Each time her head jerked back up, her heart fell again.

Maggie shifted her position a bit to try to relieve the
pain in her lower back. As she did, the man got up and
walked to the kitchen counter and checked his phone. He'd
gone through their chargers earlier, until finally finding

that Kyle's fit his phone, and had plugged his phone in a few hours earlier. An hour later, the power had gone out.

The man had demanded to know where Maggie's candles were, then had lit a few emergency candles and put them on saucers on the kitchen counter. Maggie had stared at them for a while, wondering how long it would take to burn through the rope on her wrists if she could get to one of them.

As the man stalked over to the sink and got a glass of water from the tap, Kyle stirred, then sat up and looked over at his mother.

"Mom," he said in a near-whisper. "I have to pee."

Maggie sighed and looked over at the man, who leaned on the counter drinking her water from one of her grandmother's canning jars.

"Kyle needs to use the bathroom," she said. "Please."

The man put a hand on his hip and stared at Kyle, who glanced over at him, then stared down at the table. Maggie hated the man more for this than she did for her broken face.

She watched as the man stalked down the hall and disappeared into the bathroom, heard him opening and closing the cabinet and the vanity drawer. After a minute or two, he came back out. By then, Sky had roused as well.

The man stood near the table and stared down at Kyle.

"Don't mistake it for kindness, boy," he said. "I don't want to smell your pee the rest of the night." He stepped behind Kyle's chair. "Get up."

Kyle stood, his legs weak and shaky from sitting so long. The man yanked at his wrists and began working the rope.

"I have to go, too," Sky said, less belligerently than she'd spoken earlier.

"You just might have to do without it," the man said. "Might teach you some manners."

Maggie watched Sky chew at the corner of her lip, a mannerism she'd inherited from Maggie, but which Maggie had never really noticed before.

The man left one side of the knot hanging loosely from Kyle's left wrist, and grabbed his shoulder. "Let's go," he said.

He pushed Kyle down the hall to the bathroom and shoved him in, pulled the door shut. He stood there and waited by the door, and a few minutes later, the toilet flushed and the man opened the door. "Come on," he said, and brought Kyle back out to the table.

Kyle's face was wet, and Maggie gave him a mental high-five for thinking to get a drink while he was in there, but there was an angry heat in her chest. Her child had to drink from the bathroom tap and ask permission to pee in his own home, from someone who would never be half the man that Kyle promised to become. If he could.

The man stopped Kyle at the chair, retied his wrists, and then pushed him back down. Then he stood there for a moment and regarded Sky, who refused to look at him.

"Get up, then," the man told her, and she struggled to her feet. He untied her wrists, and she rubbed at them for a moment, the rope hanging from her left wrist, before the man yanked her away from the table and followed her down the hall.

He waited outside the bathroom again, and after the toilet flushed, he waited a moment for her to open the door, then opened it himself. "Hold up," Maggie heard the man say.

"I don't have anything," Sky said after a moment, and Maggie realized he'd been checking her pockets. A moment later, they came back into the main room, Sky in the lead.

Maggie watched the man retie her daughter's bonds. Sky sat up straight, stiff as a board, but Maggie saw her wince as the ropes were cinched around her small wrists. Then the man looked over at her.

"Come on," he said. He bent down and grabbed her under the arm, and pulled her up as she clumsily got her footing. The man looked her in the eye. "I'll put a bullet in this boy's head if you come out of there with so much as a Q-Tip, you hear?"

Maggie stared back at him, and he jerked Kyle back up out of his chair and pulled the .22 from the back of his jeans, then jerked his head toward the hall. Maggie walked past them, and the man followed.

As they neared the bathroom door, Maggie heard snuffling underneath her door, followed by scratching and a small whimper.

"It's okay, Coco," she said, and her voice was hoarse, her throat sticky and sore. Coco whined a reply and sniffed the crack again, then Maggie heard a thump on the door as the dog laid down against it.

When she got to the bathroom doorway, she stopped and turned. The man stepped forward and made a circling motion with his free hand, the .22 right up against Kyle's temple. Maggie turned around to face the bathroom.

The man began untying her rope. It took a bit of time with one hand. "You got one minute to do your business and get out," he said.

Maggie had little feeling in her wrists and hands. She only knew her hands were loose when her shoulders relaxed and her arms fell to her side. The man pushed her into the bathroom and shut the door behind her.

Maggie hadn't realized she needed to use the restroom until Kyle had asked, but now she was desperate to do so. She'd had several cups of coffee and glasses of iced tea that day, and hadn't used the bathroom since before she'd called Wyatt.

As her numb fingers fumbled with her khaki shorts, Maggie pictured Wyatt asleep in his hotel room, and wished that she were curled up behind him. Actually, she wished that all three of them were.

She finally got her shorts down and sat just in time. As she emptied her bladder, a thousand hot needles began piercing her hands and wrists. She ignored them, and tried to think if there was anything at all in the bathroom that could help her.

She ran through a mental inventory and came up empty. Her and Sky's razors were packed. Even the big nail clippers were tucked inside her toiletry bag. She didn't even have some bleach or other cleaner to throw in his face.

She cleaned herself and got her shorts buttoned and her belt buckled, then flushed the toilet. The door opened even as the water was still swirling down the pipes. Maggie flexed and stretched her hands for a moment, relishing the movement, then he jerked his head and she stepped out into the hall. The man gestured at her to turn around again and she did, but not before she swore she got a faint whiff of Kyle's shampoo.

"Pull them pockets out," he said. Maggie turned her front pockets inside out, and they poked up like rabbit's ears from her shorts. Then the man patted her back pockets with his free hand, ran his hand along the inside of her waistband.

"Go on, sit back at the table," he said.

Maggie preceded them into the dining area and sat back down at the end of the table. She caught Sky's eye, and hated seeing a look of resignation on her face that hadn't been there earlier.

The man sat Kyle back down, then walked over to Maggie and stood beside her chair. He seemed to be thinking, unsure of his next step. "Put those hands through the chair there," he said. Maggie considered this. This was the last moment she'd have her hands free, but trying to take him would get her shot and do nothing to free her children. She put her hands through the spindles on the back of her chair.

The man tucked his gun into his waistband and bent to grab her rope. For a moment, Maggie mentally measured the space between her hands and his waistband. He wasn't especially tall, but he was too tall for her to snatch the gun, even if she could move faster than he could see. Even so, the nearness of it was almost irresistibly compelling.

"Can I sit by my Mom?' Kyle asked.

The man had just wound the second loop around Maggie's other wrist, and he straightened up enough to look over Maggie's shoulder at her son. Maggie moved her wrists just a tiny bit apart and balled her hands into fists.

"You a mama's boy, kid?"

Maggie's heart nearly broke as Kyle lifted his chin. "No," he said quietly. "I just want to sit by my Mom."

"We got a girl thinks she can mouth off to a full-grown man and a boy that wants to sit by his Mommy," the man said. He continued tying Maggie's wrists as he smirked at Kyle.

"Leave him alone," Sky said. "He's just a little kid."

"Aw. That's real nice," the man said. "It's good that you got a girl who can stand up for you, kid."

Maggie wanted to head butt him. She wanted to scream at him for insulting her child. But more than that, she wanted him to ignore her, so she sat silently, hoping her kids would forgive her for not speaking up for them.

"You think you're a badass because you hit women and terrorize little kids?" Sky asked.

"I think I'm a badass because I got a gun," the man said.

He finished tying Maggie's wrists and straightened, jerked his hand at the kids. "Go on, switch seats. I don't care. Be closer to your mama, boy, in case you need to nurse."

Sky and Kyle got to their feet and edged around each other to change chairs. Once they had sat back down, the man walked over to the kitchen and opened up the fridge. He pulled out another Dr. Pepper, opened it, then wandered over to the counter by the sink, where he had dumped Maggie's gym bag.

Maggie watched him as he unzipped the bag and pulled out her .45 and inspected it like he was at a gun show. As he did, she un-balled her fists and twisted her wrists. It wasn't much more wiggle room, but it was just enough for her to stretch her middle finger to the overhand knot he'd used to "lock" the loops around her wrists.

Again, she wondered why he'd used such an inefficient knot. It was likely that he'd just made the best of the rope he had, as best he knew. The men she grew up with were all fishermen of some kind, though, and she knew enough to know that there were several marine knots that would have been better.

Maybe he was a landlubber. Maybe he liked sex games and the handcuff knot was all he knew. Whatever the case, she was grateful. She wasn't sure she could untie the overhand knot with one finger, but she had a better chance than if he'd known what he was doing.

CHAPTER
EIGHT

aggie picked at the overhand knot for what felt like hours, but probably wasn't. With the windows boarded, she had lost confidence in her sense of time.

Her hands, like her, were small, and her fingers short and deceptively delicate for a woman who could work the oyster beds and fire several weapons accurately. Her middle finger wasn't quite long enough for her to gain any purchase underneath the overhand knot, so somewhere along the way she'd switched to picking at the threads of the rope itself to try to dig herself something that she *could* manipulate.

If she could get the simple overhand knot loose, the handcuff knot itself would become expandable and she could be free. To do something she wasn't sure of yet.

Sky and Kyle dropped in and out of sleep, and Maggie herself nodded off for a few minutes at a time. She was groggy and she was slightly nauseous, and she wondered if she had a mild concussion from either the gun butt to the head or her fall on the stairs.

The man, too, had slept for a few minutes here and there, his chin falling to his chest before he jerked it up again and quickly checked to make sure she was still where he'd left her.

At one point, she had found herself trying once more to engage the man in conversation, more to keep herself awake than anything else.

After looking over at the kids to make sure they were asleep, she had quietly cleared her throat, and he'd looked over at her.

"Why don't you just take me outside and shoot me? Why sit here all night? You could just be done with it and walk back to town."

His upper lip had curled just slightly, like she'd put a plate of salad in front of him when he'd asked for a steak. For some moments, she'd thought he was going to ignore her again, but then he spoke.

"Because I ain't here for me. I'm here on someone else's part," he'd said.

"Whose?" she'd asked, though she hadn't really expected an answer.

He'd glanced over at the kids before he replied. "You'll know that soon enough," he'd said, then he'd tried to make his call for the hundredth time.

He'd slapped the phone down after a few seconds. "Damn storm."

Then he had walked over to look at her bookshelves again, and she'd gone back to her rope.

⚓ ⚓ ⚓

Maggie hadn't realized that she'd dropped off again until the noise woke her. The plywood was wrenched violently from the kitchen window, then banged against the side of the house as it was blown away.

Apparently, the man had fallen asleep at some point, too, for both he and Maggie jerked their heads up, and he jumped out of his chair. He looked just as surprised as she was to see daylight. Somehow, Maggie had started to believe it would always be night.

As the man looked out of the kitchen window, the kids roused, and Maggie checked her rope. She had managed to dig herself a ragged little hole in one part of the overhand knot, but she hadn't yet managed to pull the knot any looser. She dug what was left of the nail of her middle finger into the niche and went back to work trying to pull it loose.

Her best hope was that once she did loosen the ties, she would have a moment while he used the bathroom or was otherwise occupied somewhere else in the house. He seldom left the main room, but he had wandered on occasion. If she were quiet enough, and fast enough, she might get to one of the weapons that he had left strewn on the kitchen counter last night. His .22 was still in his waistband, and she wondered why he didn't just switch it out for her Glock. She would.

He turned away from the kitchen window and wandered down the hall to the bathroom, walked in without shutting the door. Maggie's stomach turned a little as she listened to him urinating a night's worth of Dr. Peppers.

She picked at the rope furiously, and almost stopped breathing for a moment when she felt the knot give just a bit. It was almost imperceptible, but it was movement. She couldn't help but huff out a little breath, and when she did, she met Sky's eye.

Wyatt shifted uncomfortably in a chair that felt as though it were made of recycled shopping carts. He'd already done his pee test, and was waiting for the nurse to draw his blood. Apparently, all of this was to save time tomorrow, when he had his surgery, but he failed to see the logic of that.

His phone vibrated in his shirt pocket, and the nurse gave his a disapproving look over her shoulder.

"Sorry," he said with a shrug. "I'll turn it off after this call." He pulled out his cell. "Hello?"

"Hey, Wyatt, it's Gray Redmond," Maggie's father said.

"Hey, Gray, how was the cruise?"

"It was great, but I was wondering if you'd heard from Maggie."

"What do you mean?"

"Well, they're not here," Gray answered. "We got in about half an hour ago, but there's no sign of them."

Wyatt frowned and looked at his watch. "Did you call her?"

"Yes, but it went straight to voice mail. I called the kids, too. Same thing."

"Maybe there's a problem with T-Mobile," Wyatt said. "They might be overloaded with the storm."

"Maybe," Gray said. "I was hoping you'd heard from her though."

"Not since last night. She called to tell me that Kyle came home early, so they were going to head out. That was about six or seven."

Gray was quiet for a minute. "Maybe we should rent another car and drive home," he said finally.

"No, don't do that," Wyatt said. "I'm sure she's fine. Maybe traffic on I-10 sucked with everybody headed inland. They may have stopped somewhere for the night and gotten behind. She's headed your way, so you should stay there."

"All right, we'll wait a bit longer. I don't suppose you could get the Highway Patrol or somebody looking for her?"

"I'm planning on it," Wyatt answered. "Don't worry, I'm sure she's fine. I'll call you as soon as I hear something."

"Same here," Gray said.

Wyatt hung up and thought a minute. He'd talked to Deputy Dwight Shultz earlier, and he knew that what remained of the Sheriff's Office and the Apalach PD were people who were busy helping with the evacuations and taking emergency calls. The National Guard had been in Apalach since before sunrise, and Apalach was being evacuated, along with several other coastal towns between Cedar Key and Biloxi.

Hurricane Faye hadn't made landfall, but she wasn't heading out to the Gulf, either. She'd just been sitting off the coast, collecting and dumping more and more rain. Between the rains and the wind, storm surges of up to six feet had begun flooding the streets along the bay.

Wyatt opened his contacts list and began scrolling, then found the number he was looking for and tapped it. It was answered on the second ring. "Brevard County Sheriff's Office, Capt. Burrell speaking."

"Hey, Paul, it's Wyatt."

"Hey, man, how's it going?" Paul answered cheerfully. "If you're looking for your old job back, I think the Sheriff's ready to let you have it."

"No, I'll keep the one I've got, thanks," Wyatt said. "But I need a favor. It's important."

"Shoot."

"One of my people was supposed to have driven over to Jax last night, and she never showed. I need you to check the accident reports."

Five minutes later, Wyatt called Gray back and at least let him know that Maggie's Cherokee hadn't been in a reported accident. After reassuring Gray that Maggie was bound to turn up shortly, he tried her number himself and got the same result Gray had. He hung up and frowned at the cracks in the tile floor for a moment.

He looked up when the nurse approached with a small tray containing a hypodermic and a couple of glass vials. He leaned on his cane and struggled to his feet.

"Mr. Hamilton? Do you need to use the restroom?"

"Actually, I'm afraid we're going to have to reschedule."

"Sir, we can't reschedule. Your surgery is tomorrow at seven."

"Yeah, we're gonna have to reschedule that, too."

Wyatt limped out of the room and went to find a taxi.

⚓ ⚓ ⚓

Maggie was picking at the threads of her rope, trying to get it to move again, when the man's cell phone rang from the kitchen counter. She actually jumped when it did, and she froze while the man ran over to the counter from the kitchen window.

"Hey!" he said when he answered. "What do you mean, where have I been? I been trying to call you all night and I couldn't get nothin' to go through." He paused and listened for a moment. "I'm at her house, with *her*! Her *and* her kids." He listened for a few seconds. "Because they were here, dammit. Now you listen to me. You get over here, and you bring me some jumper cables."

He rubbed at his face as he listened for a moment. Maggie started picking faster and harder. When she glanced across the table, she saw that Sky was watching her.

"I don't care about no evacuations," the man said. "My truck is dead and I need you to get over here now, and bring me cables! How many—" He glanced over his shoulder, then lowered his voice a little. "How many times did you say you wanted payback for your son? Well, I'm handing it to you. So get over here."

Maggie stared at him as he slapped the phone shut and leaned on the counter. She even stopped picking at her knot for a moment.

She glanced over at Kyle. He looked out of it, dazed. She didn't know how much of that was exhaustion, hunger and dehydration, and how much of it was resignation and fear. Sky's demeanor had also become more fearful. It was amazing how fast a person's spirit could be worn down. The teenager's chin wasn't quite so high, and her eyes were still watchful but no longer defiant.

The man turned around and walked lazily over to the table and leaned on one hand. Maggie could feel the warm air from his mouth and she tried not to breathe anything of him into her lungs.

"I'd do some praying, if I was you," he said, grinning. "It looks like your comeuppance has come up."

He patted her on the head like she was a neighbor's puppy, then walked back into the kitchen. He stood with his back to her at the kitchen sink, and watched as the branches on the tree just outside bent at impossible angles.

Maggie was staring at a spot between his shoulder blades when the rope gave again, just a tiny bit, but enough to dig her nail into. She cut her eyes over to Sky. The girl was staring at the table, and Maggie sniffed.

When Sky looked up, Maggie touched her chin to her right shoulder. Sky just stared, and Maggie did it again. Sky eyes moved to Maggie's shoulder, and Maggie lifted it. Just barely, but visibly. She saw Sky blink a couple of times, then Maggie tried winking at her, and she could see that Sky finally got the message that Maggie was either loose or working on it.

Maggie glanced over at the man's back again before looking at Sky and nodding. She almost came undone when Sky's eyes filled with tears.

⚓   ⚓   ⚓

Boudreaux closed his cell phone when he heard the call disconnect, then turned it over a few times in his hand as he stared at the stone surface of the kitchen island.

"Who the phone?" Miss Evangeline snapped from the kitchen table. It took Boudreaux a moment to hear her, and he turned around.

"Something's come up," he said.

She pointed her thick lenses at him, and the flame from the hurricane lamp on the counter reflected in both of them. "I know somethin' come up," she barked. "Hurricane come up, like I done told you."

Boudreaux looked over at Amelia, who was toasting a slice of bread for her mother over one of the gas burners. "I'm going to have to go out for a bit," he said quietly.

"What you mean, go out?' Amelia asked. "Ain't no 'out' out there."

"Flood come up, too, like I told you," Miss Evangeline piped up. "Water come all up Mr. Benny yard like I say."

Boudreaux turned around and looked at her. "Yes, Miss Evangeline, you were right," he said politely. "I was wrong. Again."

"Wrong, right don't matter, no," she said, but she looked satisfied anyway. "Matter that the shark gon' be in the yard, eatin' all the drown cats and messin' round my mango."

Boudreaux sighed. It had taken him hours yesterday to convince Miss Evangeline to come stay in the house with him. The house was elevated on a brick foundation, while the cottage in back was not. Miss Evangeline had wanted to stay back there and guard her TV set against sharks and looters. The only reason she'd finally come was that he'd pointed out how much dear Lily would hate the idea of Amelia and Miss Evangeline sleeping in the guest room.

He looked back at Amelia, who had turned off the burner and was sliding the toast onto a saucer. "I won't be long," he said. "Just stay put and you'll both be fine. I'll be back as soon as I can."

"But where you goin'?" she asked.

"Who go?" Miss Evangeline snapped.

"He say he goin' somewhere," Amelia said.

Boudreaux sighed as he heard Miss Evangeline's chair bumping against the floor. He turned around to find her grabbing onto her walker and standing.

"Mr. Benny ain't go nowhere!" she said. "I ain't gon' tolerate no nonsense, me."

"I'll be back in just a few minutes," he lied, trying to sound soothing to someone who hadn't been soothed once in almost a hundred years.

She jabbed a bent finger at him. "Where you think you got to go in the hurricane?"

He took a breath and let it out slowly. "To Maggie Redmond's."

"No. I won't have none of this," she said, and started inching toward the hallway that led to the front door. "You need stay right where you at, and you get your mind off that girl. I told you leave it alone, me!"

Boudreaux watched her head out the kitchen doorway at what would have been breakneck speed for someone whose neck was already broken. Boudreaux supposed she was going to head him off at the pass. He looked at Amelia. "Go make sure she doesn't unlock that door," he said.

Amelia sighed and put down the saucer, then went after her mother. Boudreaux dropped his cell phone into his trouser pocket and heard it tap against the switchblade he'd carried every day for forty years. Then he headed for the back door. On his way, he could hear Miss Evangeline in the hallway.

"You think you go somewhere," she was saying. "You try and I put my foot to that Cajun ass."

oudreaux saw with some frustration that the few remaining late season mangoes had been stripped from the full-size trees, and that the wind was beating the hydrangea, bougainvillea, and hibiscus bushes to death. The smaller, potted mangoes had been moved to the brick potting house, and he hoped they were faring better.

The water in the yard was shin deep, and branches, small garden pots, and unfamiliar debris from other yards swept across his path as he made his way to the garage.

He had to use the key to open the door to the garage where he kept his hunting truck, a Ford F450 that had been lifted and set upon oversize tires for mucking through Tate's Hell Forest. It was overkill, but he occasionally enjoyed a little overkill.

It took him a minute to work the key underwater, then he pulled up the door. The garage, too, was flooded, and he sloshed to the truck, glad for a brief respite from the wind and the rain. He was already soaked, despite grabbing his yellow raincoat and, at 45mph, the rain felt like broken glass.

He started the Ford and pulled to the end of the driveway as a five-ton National Guard truck with a green cargo cover pulled to a stop just in front of him. A blond soldier in his early twenties leaned out the open passenger side window. Boudreaux rolled down his window and winced against the rain.

"Sir, can I ask where you're headed?"

"Well, I was a little too stubborn last night, but I'm evacuating now," he answered.

"Is it just you, sir?"

"Yes, sir," Boudreaux said pleasantly. "The rest of the family left yesterday."

"Well, there's bad flooding all along 98 on the bay, so we're directing everyone left to take 12th Street to Bluff Road and on to the airport," the man said. "We've got shelters set up there for you."

"That's where I'm headed," Boudreaux said. "Bluff Road." Lying was always easier when it was mostly truth.

"Very good, sir. Good luck," the man said, and the truck moved on, slowly making its way along Avenue D.

Boudreaux pulled out onto the street and turned left, away from the Guard truck, to head for 12th Street and Bluff Road. Maggie's road.

⚓ ⚓ ⚓

Wyatt waited at the checkout counter at the car rental agency, leaning on his cane for balance as the young redheaded girl with the impossibly bright smile tapped away at her keyboard.

"And you'll just be using the car locally?" she asked.

"Yes," he lied, and felt bad about that, but he was pretty sure that if he said he was driving over to the Gulf Coast, she wouldn't give him the keys.

She tapped a few more keys. "Okay, we can give you the Florida resident, local only rate of $29.99 per day, with a free upgrade to a mid-size sedan. Does that sound good?"

"That sounds great, thanks," he said, and looked at his watch.

"Here's your license, Mr. Hamilton, and I'll just print out your agreement for you to sign."

Wyatt put the license back in his wallet and tried Maggie's cell one more time. Nothing. He slid the phone back into his shirt pocket.

"Here you go, Mr. Hamilton," the redhead said. "If you'll just sign where indicated and check the boxes that are highlighted, we'll have your car brought around front."

Wyatt got everything signed and checked, and smiled and said "thank you" where indicated as well, but he had a hard time not rapping the cane against the counter and asking her to speed things along.

Finally, she handed him seven copies of his rental agreement in three different pastel colors, and pointed at the glass front doors. "There's your car now," she said. "We'll see you back here tomorrow."

"Okee-doke," Wyatt said, and lurched toward the doors.

He knew that, most likely, Maggie had had car trouble or some other minor issue that had prevented her leaving Apalach as scheduled. He also knew that, given the fact that one of them had been shot every time they tried to have a real date, it wasn't that outrageous to assume she'd simultaneously had phone trouble. He just wasn't sure he was buying it.

If he drove through hell and high water, pissed off his doctors, and was popping Percocet tonight all because she forgot to gas up the Jeep or something, he'd go ahead and yell at her for a while, then make her cook him a steak. Maybe he'd even take her dog.

Until then, he was going to assume that there was a good reason for him to be doing what he was doing.

⚓　⚓　⚓

When Maggie felt the rope actually give, truly and without question move, she immediately broke into a sweat.

It wasn't that she was exerting herself any more than she had been; it was the almost instantaneous supply of adrenaline her brain provided her heart and muscles as soon as it perceived that she had a reason to need it.

Her mouth opened just a bit, and her eyes widened, and she saw immediately that Sky noticed. Sky had been watching her for the last half hour, alternating staring at her mother with glancing over at the man, who seemed newly enervated by the promise of the new arrival. He had been walking around the main room without purpose, occasionally stopping to check his phone, get a drink of water, or watch the storm out the kitchen window.

Maggie purposefully and with great effort kept her breathing slow and even, and kept her butt in her chair and her arms back, though every instinct but the smart ones pushed her to leap from her chair.

What she wished was for the man to go to the bathroom, go anywhere that would give her half a chance at getting to one of her guns on the kitchen counter. But she knew that she would be unlikely to have enough time to get there, reload one of the guns he'd emptied, and be ready before he shot her in the back.

The man walked over to the front door and laid his ear against it, listening. Maggie heard nothing but the incessant wind and rain.

Her focus changed to the gun that was already loaded, the one tucked into the front of his waistband. She needed that gun.

She was taking slow, deep breaths, trying to slow her thoughts so that she could come up with something viable, when Sky got up out of her chair, wobbling a little unsteadily on cramped legs.

"I need to pee," she said boldly.

The man straightened up and snarled at her. "No, you don't. Sit back down."

"Sky!" Kyle croaked.

"No! You wanna kill me, you ignorant redneck, then you go ahead and do it, but they're not gonna find me with piss running down my leg," Sky snapped. "Take me to the freaking bathroom."

Maggie's heart pounded with hope as the man shot over to the table, but he pulled out the .22 and pointed it at Sky's face. "Sit down now," he said through his teeth. Maggie's eyes zoomed in on the safety, expecting him to flick it off at any moment.

Sky's eyes blinked several times, but when she opened her mouth, all she said was, "No."

"Sky!" Kyle yelled again, and Coco started barking furiously from the bedroom.

The man kipped the gun sideways and pulled his arm back a bit to strike Sky with it, and Maggie stopped thinking.

She grabbed the loose rope in her right hand and whipped the remaining knot off of her left wrist as she got to her feet. She had been planning on slapping at the gun with it, but as she got up, she changed her angle. It was unplanned and awkward, and she was slower than she had been when she'd envisioned it in her mind.

She slung it underhand, hitting him where his wrist met his hand. She was unsteady on her feet and her head spun a little, so she didn't have the momentum she'd hoped she would, but it was enough to knock the gun from his hand. It clattered to the table, then skidded off the table and onto the wood floor, where it slid under the kitchen island.

Sky sat down hard in surprise as the man whipped his head to follow the trajectory of his gun, then spun back to face Maggie. Maggie got one kick to the back of his thigh, but she had to use her left leg and wasn't really positioned for good leverage. The kick was slightly weak and put her off balance, but it was hard enough and well placed enough to make him slump a bit.

As he did, Maggie stepped forward and got him in the throat with the side of her left hand. It was a hit, but a weaker hit than she needed it to be. The pain registered on his face, but when she went for an upper cut with her right fist, he caught it.

She twisted out of it before he could break her wrist, but his free hand popped straight at her and he slammed her broken nose with his palm. Pain exploded in every part of her face and head, and her vision swam. It gave him the precious few seconds he needed to wrap both hands around her throat.

Maggie heard both Kyle and Sky screaming behind her as the man bent her backwards over the table. She thrust her arms between his and outward against his elbows in an attempt to break his hold, but she didn't have the speed or power behind it that she needed.

He actually lifted her by her neck, stronger than he'd appeared to be, and slammed her down on the table on her back. For a moment, Kyle's face was visible above her, just inches away. She grabbed both of his thumbs and started trying to bend them backwards, to twist them enough to make him loosen his grip, but she couldn't breathe and her vision was already darkening.

Maggie kept pulling back on the man's thumbs, trying to dislodge his hands from her throat just enough to get one breath of air, one breath to keep her conscious. The man lifted her neck just a few inches and slammed her head against the tabletop. She heard Kyle screaming, could see his frightened eyes just a few inches above her, as he sat there, staring down in horror.

She felt her brain start to shut down, and she thought, *Please don't choke me to death six inches away from my son. Please don't do this in front of my children.*

Above the sound of her children's screaming and the man's cursing, she heard the front door slam inward. It crashed against the wall with a clap as loud as thunder, and suddenly wind filled the room, and rain fell onto Maggie's legs where they twisted and kicked between the man's.

Then, like something her air-starved brain had conjured, Boudreaux's face appeared over the man's shoulder. He was looking at her, and the pure, unadulterated, animalistic rage in his bright blue eyes was like something from someone else's nightmare.

Maggie didn't even have time to reconcile what she was seeing with what she thought ought to be there. Boudreaux's arm whipped around the man's neck, and the man released Maggie's throat. Two seconds later, they were both gone. Boudreaux pulled the man backwards, back out the front door, and the wind yanked the door shut again with a bang.

It was as though some huge, tentacled creature had wrapped itself around a sailor and pulled him overboard into the sea, just like that. If she couldn't still feel the rain on her legs, couldn't see the water all over the floor in front of the door as she pushed herself up on one arm, Maggie

would not have believed that it had actually happened the
way her eyes told her that it had.

CHAPTER
TEN

Maggie laid on the table for two pounding heartbeats, then slid off and onto her feet, and scrambled over to Sky's chair.

"Mom, what just happened?" Sky asked, her voice near hysterical.

"I don't know," Maggie managed to croak, squatting behind Sky's chair and furiously working the ropes that bound her wrists.

"What did he do?"

"I don't know, Sky!"

The wind was whistling like a train outside, and it seemed impossible that it could be louder than it had already been. Maggie looked up toward the kitchen window as something small but hard hit it, and she caught Kyle's eye. He was staring at the front door, his eyes wide.

"I'm coming, Kyle," Maggie said. He looked at her, but didn't say anything.

Sky wiggled her fingers. "Hurry, Mom!"

"Hold still, baby, please," Maggie said.

She yanked the ropes free and jumped up as Sky pulled her arms around to the front. They were stiff from hours of being bound behind her, and she rolled them gingerly.

"Sky, I need you to grab the Glock," Maggie said, as she squatted behind Kyle and started working on the ropes. His thin wrists were bleeding, and the ropes had left welts on them that made Maggie want to scream.

Sky ran over to the kitchen counter and picked up the Glock, where it lay with the Mossberg and her great-grandfather's .38. "Do you want me to bring it to you?"

"No, I need it for you," she said. "Do you remember how to use it?"

"Yeah, but…I guess. Why not the .38?"

"This is not the time for a revolver, baby," Maggie answered. "Just take it. I want you take it, and I want you to take Kyle, and I want you guys to go in my room, and you don't come out unless I come get you."

"Mom, wait—"

"You don't come out unless I come get you, do you understand me?" Maggie yelled.

"Yes."

A branch slammed into the window behind Sky, and she ducked instinctively, but the glass didn't break. The branch fell away again as she straightened up and grabbed the extra rounds from the counter and shoved them into her pocket.

Maggie finally pulled Kyle's wrists free, and she rubbed them for just a second before she pulled him up from the chair. "Kyle, you go with Sky, and you guys stay in there. Do you hear me?"

"Yeah," he said, his voice a croak.

"Go!" Maggie barked at Sky, and the kids ran down the hallway. As soon as she heard their steps, Coco started barking and scratching at the door again. Maggie watched

Sky open the door, watched the kids go in and slam the door behind them, then she ran over to the kitchen counter.

She glanced up at the front door several times, as she loaded the Mossberg, shoved a couple of extra rounds in her shorts pocket, and then ran over to the door. The floor was wet from when he had burst through, and she slipped and nearly went down before catching herself.

She put an ear to the door, but it was a ridiculous thing to do. On the other side was nothing but noise, and she could hear nothing beyond the pounding of the rain on the deck.

She took a deep breath, slammed back the action on the shotgun, and flung open the door.

Boudreaux was in the yard, a few feet from the bottom of the stairs. He was almost knee deep in water from the creek, and the water closest to him was colored a deep, dark red.

He looked up at her, the wind buffeting him and pushing him, his hair whipping wildly.

Maggie raised the shotgun and felt a catch in her throat as she looked into those eyes, so deeply blue even from this distance. She hadn't wanted him to be the one, and she felt, ridiculously, the heaviness of disappointment in her chest.

"I wish you hadn't come here, Mr. Boudreaux."

He stared at the shotgun, then wiped his forearm across his eyes. "Your father called me," he yelled to her above the rain and wind.

It took a second for Maggie to process what he'd said. "What?"

"He was worried about you," he called back.

"Why would he call you?" she demanded.

Boudreaux seemed to hesitate for a moment. She could almost see him deciding on the best answer. "Because he knew I would come," he yelled.

Maggie raised the shotgun just a hair. "That doesn't—" she started, but then she heard a whining, almost keening sound, like someone slashing a bow across the strings of a violin, and a section of sheet metal or aluminum, maybe a piece of someone's storage shed, came whipping through the air.

Boudreaux turned to look when she did, but it wasn't soon enough to get out of its way. It banged into and across him at the midsection, then was flung into the water beside him, where it was quickly carried away in the fast-moving water.

When Maggie looked back at Boudreaux, he had his mouth open as though he was about to say something, and then, all at once, his white button-down shirt was flooded with red, red that soaked the shirt from the inside, just above his waist, from one hip to the other, with remarkable speed.

Boudreaux didn't seem to notice it until he saw her face, then he looked down and placed a palm on his stomach.

Maggie opened her mouth to yell a warning as a fresh surge from the creek cascaded into the yard, carrying with it clumps of debris. In an instant, the water was above Boudreaux's knees, and just as he looked up at Maggie, part of an old railroad tie bumped into his leg and Boudreaux went to his knees.

The water pushed him over to one side, then face first into the swirl, all in the span of just a few seconds. Maggie took one step toward the stairs, then froze as she saw Boudreaux get swept away toward the chicken yard, then disappear altogether beneath the water.

She turned around and ran back into the house, skidding on the now much larger puddle in front of the door. She looked around for a moment, then spotted the man's cell phone on the kitchen counter and ran over to it.

She flipped open the phone, tapped his call log and looked at the number he'd dialed 17 times. She didn't recognize it. She tapped it, and it was answered on the first ring.

"I still got an hour of driving," a woman's raised voice said. "I'm going as fast as I can!"

"Who is this?" Maggie asked evenly.

There was a long pause before the woman's rough voice came back across the line. "Who is *this*?" She sounded panicked.

"Maggie Redmond," Maggie answered.

"You murdered our son, you whore!" the woman yelled. "You killed my Richard!"

Maggie let out a slow breath. Ricky Alessi. This crazy woman had raised the meth dealer who'd tried to kill Maggie, and now she was raising poor Grace's kids. She was about to ask where they were when the woman yelled at her.

"Where's Dewitt?"

"Giving an account of himself to God," Maggie said. "You want to be next, Mrs. Alessi? Keep coming. I'll blow a hole in you big enough for me to crawl through."

"You evil little—" the woman's scream was cut off and there was nothing. Maggie looked at the phone. It was dead. She allowed herself one second to be furious at herself for wasting the last few seconds of its battery life, then slammed the phone down on the counter.

Maggie spun around and nearly trod upon Stoopid, who had come into the kitchen to give her an update on the weather, their situation, or his desire to be fed. "Move,

Stoopid!" Maggie snapped, as she hopped over him, and he turned and flailed onto to the bottom rail of the kitchen island.

Maggie ran back out onto the deck, shutting the door behind her to keep Stoopid from running outside.

She scanned the front and left side yards for a few moments, constantly wiping the rain from her face, before she spotted a flash of white over by the garden.

Boudreaux was hung up against one of the raised beds. He was partially on his side, one elbow up on the topmost railroad tie, but his face was in the water.

Maggie half ran, half slid down the deck stairs and jumped into the water. It was up to the bottom of her backside, and she was amazed at how powerfully it pushed against her legs. They'd had flooding before, but not like this, not this deep and this fast-moving. Not in her memory.

She had to alternate wading with the current and dragging her feet in order to remain standing, but she still came close to falling several times, as she stumbled against a rock or a hump in the dirt. At one point, something slammed against her calves, and she almost went down.

She had to stop periodically, turn her body, and force her way diagonally toward the garden again, as the water sought to push her past it. She had a vision of herself, running against her will with the water, into the woods and on out to the river beyond them.

She finally reached Boudreaux, and she tried to brace herself against the raised bed with one hip as she bent down and turned him over. His eyes were closed.

"Boudreaux!" she yelled over the noise of the storm. It was the first time in her life that she hadn't addressed him as 'Mr.'

"Get up!" she yelled at him, pulling on the shoulders of his shirt. His eyelids fluttered a moment, then he opened his eyes. He didn't seem to see her at first.

"Move! I need you to get up!"

He finally focused on her, raised one arm up out of the water and pointed beyond her. "Get inside," he said, and she read his lips more than she actually heard it.

She leaned away from the raised bed, tried to plant her feet on the slick ground, and bent to slide her wrists under his arms. "Get the hell up!" she yelled again.

He struggled to get his feet underneath him, as she struggled to pull him upward without losing her own footing. The water was tugging at her lower legs like a thousand insistent toddlers, and she knew that if one foot left the ground, they both would.

Once she got Boudreaux to his feet, she was thrown for a moment by the sight of his midsection. His shirt, still mostly tucked in, had been rent almost from one side of his waist to the other. She wanted to spread the fabric open to the see the wound, but she was afraid she'd find it discouraging and that this would only distract her from getting him to the house. The amount of blood, and the fact that it was still seeping through the shirt and had soaked the top of his trousers, let her know all she really needed to know at this point: the help he needed was beyond her limited training.

"Where's your phone?" she yelled over the wind.

He had one arm draped over her neck, and raised the hand of the other one to pat his empty shirt pocket, then shook his head at her.

"Never mind. Let's go," she said.

She'd thought moving with the water was difficult. She could see immediately that working against it was going to be much harder. The house was very slightly uphill from the chicken yard and garden area, which she supposed helped make the flow so fast. She also knew that the water was not only making its way downhill, but also back to its own source. Several hundred yards through the woods in back, the river curved around and made its way to what would eventually, in five miles or so, be Scipio Creek, and then the bay.

Maggie had always loved that she had water on both one side and the back of her land, but at the moment, the flood water on her property was essentially connecting the two, and this wasn't a good thing. One way or another, everything was going to flow to the river, whether it wanted to or not.

CHAPTER
ELEVEN

Maggie bent at the waist, leaned into the wind and took the first step back toward the house. It had occasionally seemed like a bit of a hike to the house from the garden or chicken yard, mainly when she was exhausted or Stoopid was throwing himself in her way in a fit of nerves or agitation. However, the hundred feet or so that she and Boudreaux now needed to traverse seemed like a great distance indeed.

Apparently, everything was far away if you needed to get there dragging a half-dead man through thigh-high water that was moving in the other direction.

The wind and the rain wanted to push them away from the house, as well, and Maggie almost appreciated the irony of her loving storms so much. She'd never had to fight one so hard. She'd always just prepared for them as much as she'd needed to, then hunkered down to wait them out and enjoy them as much as she could.

She'd always felt somewhat guilty and secretive about her love of bad weather, especially after storms like Katrina, but she couldn't help welcoming a good pounding rain, or the rumble of thunder overhead. Some part of her mind that wasn't preoccupied with survival wondered now if she would lose that pleasure.

Boudreaux spoke to her a few times as they fought their way toward the house, but his words were lost in the wind, and overwritten by her single-minded focus on moving forward. Every time Maggie looked up at the deck stairs, she felt like they should be closer than they were, but they were at least making progress.

Maggie could feel her legs trembling from the strain, and this seemed incongruous with all of the hours that she had spent in her lifetime, running out into the ocean against the surf. She'd always loved bodysurfing, and she and her parents, and she and David, had spent countless days at Fort Walton Beach or Destin, running out into the surf, then riding it back in, from sunrise to sunset, almost without rest.

How was it that the same legs she'd had then were trying to let her down now, after just a few minutes of work? If the situation weren't so serious, she might have laughed at the idea that she could handle the surf at Orange Beach, but couldn't handle the surf in her own front yard.

When Maggie felt her foot hit the old brick fire pit, she knew they were getting close, but looking up into the rain was excruciating and nearly pointless, so she kept her head down, and she and Boudreaux stumbled into it and stepped over the other side.

It was then that Maggie heard someone yell "Mom," though it seemed to come from a long way away.

She looked up and squinted into the liquid needles, and her heart flipped over a few times. Sky and Kyle were on the deck stairs, standing at the water line, about three steps up. Sky had tied together the ropes that had been used to bind their wrists, then tied one end to the bottom of one of the balusters.

"Get back inside!" Maggie yelled, and it seemed pointless. She could almost feel her voice whipping past her own ears and into the woods behind her.

Sky either heard her anyway, or chose to look up at that moment. "Mom!" she yelled. She was hurriedly tying a bowline knot at the loose end of the rope to make a loop.

"Get inside!" Maggie yelled. She and Boudreaux were only about fifteen feet from the stairs, but it seemed like a mile, and the water wanted to push them along the side of the house and to the back. She felt as though she were pushing against an automatic door that wanted to shut itself.

Sky ignored Maggie and, one hand gripping the loop she'd made, she jumped into the water. It nearly pushed her off of her feet, but she managed to right herself, and once the rope had played out to its full six feet or so, she stretched her free arm out to her mother.

The idea that Sky would not be out of the water until she was spurred Maggie on, and she pushed against the water with her legs. She wouldn't look away from Sky long enough to look at Boudreaux, but since she felt like she was dragging him, she thought he must have fallen unconscious.

She did glance beyond Sky to Kyle, and the sight of him standing on the stairs, gripping the rail with both hands as the wind and rain whipped at him, was terrifying but mobilizing at the same time. She would get there, and she would get the kids back into the safety of the house, and after she had clutched them to her, she would scream at them.

Suddenly, the water was higher, reaching Maggie's waist, even though she knew she was moving to higher ground with every step. She looked up, and saw that the water seemed to be moving faster, as well. Her brain was still working this out when she saw her Jeep begin to move forward.

It took a second for what she was seeing to fully register. The Jeep was slowly moving toward the deck stairs. Kyle saw it, too, and looked over at her, his eyes impossibly wide. Maggie saw him turn as though to run up the stairs and she screamed at him.

"Kyle, jump!"

Kyle was an amazing kid. He was kind and he was funny and he was incredibly smart, but if Maggie could change one thing about his character or behavior, it would be his tendency to be so distracted that she had to repeat commands several times before he acted on them.

This one time, she didn't have to.

If Maggie had had time to thank God, she would have done it as she watched Kyle leap from the bottom of the stairs into the water. He was almost shoulder deep when he landed, but landed not too far behind Sky, who already had a hand stretched out to him. The water started to push him past her, but he grasped her hand and swung around in front of her before he found his footing. Then the Jeep bumped into the staircase.

Even at the slow pace it was traveling, between the water and the one loose piling, the Jeep's impact was enough to take the stairs down. Maggie and Sky watched them tumble, watched the railing tilt over sideways before breaking in two and falling over into the water.

As they did, Maggie saw Sky's arm jerk violently, and realized Sky was still holding the length of rope.

"Sky, let go!" she yelled, and Sky looked at her hand like it was someone else's, then let go of the rope. The portion of railing that the rope had been tied to spun towards the kids, then past them, nearly clipping Maggie on its way toward the garden.

The truck seemed to stop for just a moment, then started sliding again. Maggie watched, mouth open, as it slid underneath the deck and bumped into one of the concrete pilings on which the house sat. She waited for her house, her memories, her dog and her rooster to come crashing down in front of her eyes, but the square pillar was solid and it was deep.

Maggie looked away from the Jeep and back to her kids, who were struggling to get their footing. She looked past them to Boudreaux's and David's trucks, still sitting where they'd been left, as far as she could judge. She didn't trust them not to go at any moment. They weren't an option for getting out of the water, even if they managed to get to them against the flow of the surge.

Maggie looked to her right, rethought a strategy she'd never actually formulated, then yelled at Sky.

"The bushes, Sky!" Sky looked at her without understanding, and Maggie waved her free arm toward a stretch of overgrown brush and Hibiscus bushes that had been a nice hedge in her grandmother's time.

Less than thirty seconds had passed since the truck had taken down the stairs, but to Maggie's legs it felt like hours. She could feel her muscles convulsing from the effort spent to remain standing, and if her kids hadn't been in the water, she might have let the water take her and hoped to end up someplace good.

She spread her feet a bit wider and tried to dig in as the water pushed her kids, stumbling, toward her. She saw that Sky had grabbed one of Kyle's wrists and she reached out for Sky's free hand.

"Don't let go of him," she yelled, as Sky grabbed her right hand. Kyle kept moving toward her, and she instinctively opened and closed her left hand, though her left arm was wrapped around Boudreaux's waist.

She felt Boudreaux's right arm lift off of her shoulders, and she didn't know if it was intentional or accidental, but she felt him push her between her shoulder blades, and the weight of him left her side as he fell backwards.

She started to turn to grab him, but then Kyle crashed into her and she just managed to grab the back of Kyle's shirt with her now free left hand, as she kept a death grip on Sky's hand with the other.

The small impact from Kyle almost knocked her off her feet, but she righted herself, and stayed standing despite Kyle accidentally kicking her shins as he got his feet underneath him. When she turned around to look for Boudreaux, he was gone.

For just a moment, Maggie wanted to try to look for him, but which of her children would she let go of to do that?

Although Sky was just at the end of her arm, Maggie yelled to be heard over the rain and the wind, which refused to let up even a little.

"We need to get to the bushes!" Maggie yelled, her voice breaking from the strain. "Try to stay on your feet, but let it take us to the bushes!"

Sky looked at her questioningly.

"The tree! We can make it to the coon tree!"

The coon tree was a huge oak that grew near the corner of the back deck. It had gotten its name due to the mama coon and three babies that had liked to climb it in the evenings a few years ago. None of the branches overhung the deck, so it wouldn't get them back up into the house, but the trunk had split decades ago, and the low "V" made it an easy tree to climb. They could at least get out of the water. If they could get to the overgrown line of bushes that ran along the back of the yard, they could use them to make their way to the tree.

The three of them, connected by cramping, white-knuckled hands, let the water push them toward the bushes, while trying to stay on their feet. This was most difficult for Kyle, for whom the water was almost chest high, but Maggie gripped his one wrist and Sky his other, and they eventually washed up against the overgrown hibiscus, volunteer oaks, and other bushes that were now half-submerged in water.

Sky got there first, and grabbed onto a thick trunk with her free hand, then Maggie let go of her hand and grabbed some branches. By silent agreement, all three of them rested there a moment once Kyle had a grip on the shrub Maggie was holding. She still held firmly to his left hand. The water passed through and around the bushes, but the growth was thick enough to keep them from being carried through.

Sky looked over at Maggie, her chest heaving, her loose bun now plastered to her head like a small, sodden animal. "I am not drowning in my own yard!" she yelled angrily at her mother.

"No, you're not," Maggie yelled back. "Just hang on, and move toward the tree."

She watched Sky reach out her left hand, grab a bunch of branches on the next bush and pull herself over, then Maggie looked over at Kyle. She moved his hand to the back of her shorts and put it on her belt. "Grab onto my belt!"

She felt the tug as he wrapped his fingers around her leather belt. "Do not let go, do you understand me?" The boy nodded. "We're going to make our way as close to the coon tree as we can, okay?"

Kyle nodded again, and Maggie used both hands to grip the branches as she followed Sky. It took several minutes, and one battle with a drowning lawn chair that Maggie didn't recognize, but they finally managed to get to the end of the line of bushes.

There was a good six feet between the last bush and the base of the old oak. Maggie and Sky stared at the space between them, and Maggie wished they still had Sky's rope. Sky turned and looked at Maggie, and Maggie tried to look like she wasn't as frightened as she was.

"You can do it, Sky," she said. "Just stay on your feet."

Sky nodded, and stepped toward the tree, still gripping her branch in her right hand. It bent beneath the water, and she didn't let go until she had to. Then she pushed toward the tree trunk and grabbed at the small hole in the "V", now underwater, where she and Kyle used to tuck apples and raisins and other treats for the raccoons.

Sky swung her left leg through the split trunk and straddled it, then scooted up the trunk a bit until she could reach the first decent branch. She grabbed it with her left hand, then leaned out just above the water and stretched out her hand. It wasn't close enough for Maggie to reach, and with Kyle hanging onto her, she was afraid they'd pull Sky out of the tree. She turned to Kyle.

"We need to switch places, baby," she yelled. She reached underwater and grabbed his wrist, pulled his hand from her belt and put it on one of the branches in front of her face. He grabbed it, and she pulled him in front of her. For the briefest moment, she buried her face in his neck, then helped him pass over to her left.

"Okay, listen," Maggie said, grabbing his right hand in her left. "I need you to get as close as you can to Sky and get her hand. I've got you, do you understand?"

Kyle nodded. "It's okay, Mom," he yelled back, his already high-pitched voice cracking with the effort.

"Okay." Maggie held his poor hand in a death grip, and watched him get as far as he could before letting go of the branch he was holding. Maggie followed, felt the weightlessness through his hand when he lost his footing, started breathing again when he got it back.

She got as far out as she could without letting go of her branch, and her and Kyle's arms were both stretched to the limit, but Sky was finally able to grab his other hand.

"I've got him, Mom! Let go!"

"Are you sure you have him?"

"Yes! Let go!"

Maggie let go of Kyle's hand, and watched without breathing as Sky swung him through the water to the trunk. He grabbed on, and scrambled up the other side of the trunk to a decent-sized branch. When he looked back at Maggie, she almost felt as though all was right with the world again, save the rain and the wind and the water.

"C'mon, Mom!" Sky yelled, and she grabbed onto a smaller branch beside her, leaned out a little bit farther, and stretched her hand just a few inches closer.

Maggie tried to plant her feet a bit more firmly before she let go of her bush. The water seemed to be moving less quickly, but there also seemed to be more of it. It was up to her waist now, and it wanted to go down to the river. The weight of it against her legs, as it kept moving toward its goal, was unbelievable. It didn't need speed; it had the power of its volume and the power of gravity.

It took two good steps, then she was able to stretch up and grab her daughter's hand. Sky swung her back toward the trunk, and then Maggie let go of her hand and pushed forward to the trunk's "V" and grabbed it. She stood inside the split and hugged the tree a moment, her head leaning against it, as she tried to let her legs recover. They shook as though she'd been running for an hour. She took a few deep breaths, then looked over at Sky.

"We need to get higher," she called out hoarsely.

CHAPTER

TWELVE

W yatt turned the windshield wipers on high as the rain began to get heavier. He was on US-19, which would eventually take him to Hwy 98, which would eventually take him straight to downtown Apalach, but eventually was starting to seem very far away.

He was one of very few drivers on this stretch of highway, which was lined on both sides by a seemingly endless forest of scrub pines. He made a mental note to never come this way at night, as he'd probably start having hallucinations, or just pull over and kill himself to avoid having to drive it much longer.

It had been raining for the last fifty miles or so, but the rain had picked up quite a bit the further west he drove. He was a good fifteen miles from the coast, and Hurricane Faye was a good ten miles from the coast in the other direction, but she was making herself known. To Wyatt, it was starting to feel like it was just the two of them there on US-19, and he was grateful when his cell phone rang.

"Hello?"

"Hey, Wyatt. It's Gray," Maggie's father said.

"Hey, Gray. Have you heard from Maggie?" Wyatt hoped Gray had, but he was all set to get pissy if she'd just shown up in Jacksonville.

"No, we haven't," Gray answered. "I was calling to see if you had."

"No," Wyatt said, sighing. "I've called a couple times. Straight to voice mail."

"Is it raining in Orlando?" Gray asked.

"I couldn't say," Wyatt said.

"Where the hell are you, son?" Gray asked quietly.

"I'm on 19, just outside Chiefland."

There was a short pause on the line.

"You're on your way to Apalach," Gray said.

"I am."

"I thought you said we should stay put."

Wyatt pulled into the right lane to avoid a branch from a scrub pine. "No, I said *you* should stay put, because she was supposed to be headed to Jax," Wyatt said.

"I see," Gray said. "And what about your surgery?"

"They'll have to have it without me," Wyatt said. "It'll be good practice."

"Maybe the airport will be clear tomorrow and you can fly back in time."

"Maybe," Wyatt said, though he had no intention of scrambling to make it. He'd simply reschedule. "I tried getting hold of Dwight and a few other people at the SO, but I'm just getting 'all circuits are busy' or somebody's voice mail."

"Well," Gray started, then paused for a moment before going on. "I got in touch with Bennett Boudreaux about an hour and a half ago, and he said he'd go check Maggie's house, but I haven't been able to reach him again. It's ring-ing; he's just not answering. I'm a little concerned about that."

Wyatt stared out the windshield a moment. "Why would you call Boudreaux?" he asked.

"Because I knew he'd be there."

That sounded simple enough, but it didn't really sound true enough. It also didn't explain why Boudreaux would care to go driving around in a hurricane. Wyatt decided to let it go, though. Maggie's parents were stressed enough.

"Wyatt?"

"Yeah."

"I'll let you focus on driving," Gray said. "But thank you. You're a good man."

"Basically, I'm an idiot," Wyatt said. "But it serves the occasion well."

"Well, drive carefully," Gray said. "We'll wait to hear from you."

"You'll know it when I know it," Wyatt said, and hung up the phone.

Freaking Boudreaux. Every time he turned around, there were Maggie and Boudreaux, connected by invisible string. It was frustrating enough to know that Maggie felt some kind of connection to or even liking for Boudreaux. But Gray was about the most straightforward and transparent man that Wyatt knew. So what the hell was up with *him* calling the local killer to check on his daughter?

⚓ ⚓ ⚓

Boudreaux's back slammed into something large and hard, and as it did, a rush of water spewed from his lungs and out his mouth, though his face was already underwater. He jerked his head sideways and brought his face out of the water, then coughed several times, but it seemed like the rain he took in and the water he brought up were about equal in volume. His back was being pressed against something, but the rushing water all around him was pulling on his legs.

He blinked a few times before he could keep his eyes open, then reached an arm out and grasped the first thing he touched. A cypress. He was hung up on an old tree. He gripped the thin cypress knee that he'd grabbed hold of and pulled himself up into more or less a seated position. He at least had his back fully against the base of the cypress, and his head out of the water. He'd get his breath and his bearings, then see if he could stand.

He couldn't see his wound, as he was submerged to the shoulders, but he knew it was bad. He was freezing, he was lightheaded and he wanted more than anything to just sleep. He knew he was probably losing a good deal of blood and was most likely in shock. There wasn't much he could do at the moment about either one.

He put his head back against the base of the cypress, closed his eyes, and took in a mouthful of rain. He held it in his mouth for a moment before swallowing, then he looked around, as though he might discern his location. It was pointless, really. He'd never been out this way much, and all he knew was that he was somewhere near Maggie's house. He also knew he had to be fairly close to the river, and that wasn't necessarily a good thing.

He needed to pull himself together and start making his way back to Maggie's property, or anyplace further away from the river, but pulling himself together suddenly seemed like it would require far too much effort.

God was punishing him, and he knew it. He'd made God angry, and now he was feeling the fruits of his sins. God the angry Father was punishing the murdering son, and the wind and the rain were his fists.

"Hail Mary, full of grace, the Lord is with thee; blessed art thou amongst women, and blessed is the fruit of thy womb, Jesus," Boudreaux said quietly. "Holy Mary, Mother of God, pray for us sinners, now and at the hour of our death. Amen."

As he started in on his next Hail Mary, he thought to himself that if he did survive this day, Miss Evangeline was going to kill him anyway, so maybe he ought to just pray for his soul.

⚓ ⚓ ⚓

Miss Evangeline stood on the front porch near the wide steps, gripping her walker with both hands as the wind blew the rain into her face. She'd torn a hole in the bottom of a black garbage bag, and pulled it over her head to cover her clothes, but the wind whipped the bag around so bad that her house dress was soaked through anyway.

The water had come up to the second step, and she looked at the places where she knew the kalancho and impatiens to be. Poor plants was gonna drown good, and Mr. Benny yard gonna be naked.

She looked back up, squinting against the rain, and peered up one side of the street and down the other, hoping to see his big truck crawling through the water. She just wanted the truck to come back, wanted him to wade through the yard and back to the house, so she could yank him up outa the water and choke his neck dead.

She remembered then, back when they lived in the old white house on Bayou Petit Caillou, a day when he was six or seven years old.

She'd had his breakfast ready by the time the sky lightened, but seen no sign at all of the boy, and he hadn't come when she called him. She wore herself out walkin' all 'round the hen house and the yard, and no Mr. Benny. Finally, while she was out in the middle of the yard, callin' and cryin', there he come up to the dock, paddling his daddy's pirogue with oars that was bigger than him.

She ran down the bank to the dock, wood clothespins rattlin' in her apron pocket, and Mr. Benny just smile up at her like nothin' bad wrong.

"What kind of crazy you are?" she yelled at him as he tied off the boat. "Why you make Miss Evangeline heart attack itself like that?"

"I wanted some redfish," he said, holdin' up a stringer of four or five fish.

"You too little be out your daddy pirogue by yourself," she said.

He squinted his blue eyes up at her and told her, "I'm almost as big as you."

She walked over to the pirogue, her slippers slappin' against the dock, and put her hands on her hips. "You thinkin' it's a good day to sass me some, then."

"But I am almost as big as you."

"You get up here 'fore I snatch you out that boat," she said, and glared at him while he got out. Then she turned and walked back up the yard, him trailin' her, with his stringer in his hand.

"Miss Evangeline, you gonna cook me these redfish for breakfast?"

"I already cook your breakfast, me. I gon' slap you senseless with them fish." She stomped as best she could in her slippers, and yanked the screen door open. "Come in the house an' don't scare Miss Evangeline no more."

To make sure he knew she was mad for true, she hadn't said not one more word to Mr. Benny 'til he had got done eatin' them fish.

Now she heard the front door open behind her, and the screen door squeak, but she ignored them, and stared out at the water until Amelia loomed over her shoulder.

"What you doin', you crazy fool?" Amelia snapped. "I about walked myself through the floor lookin' all over this house for you!"

Miss Evangeline straightened her shoulders and stared out at the street. "I been right here," she said.

"You need come in the house," Amelia said.

"I ain't goin' nowhere 'til Mr. Benny come back here," Miss Evangeline snapped.

"He come back, you be dead from pneumonia, and he shoot me in my face," Amelia said. "Look at you. Your house dress all soak through, and your slipper drench, too."

"You go inside. I gon' wait right here 'til that fool come home."

"He come up that driveway, see you standin' out here in a garbage bag, he gon' lose his mind."

"He done lose it already," Miss Evangeline said.

"You wanna do somethin', you come back in the house and pray for him," Amelia countered, taking her mother's elbow.

"I been prayin', "Miss Evangeline said. "Prayin' he don't come up wrong 'gainst the juju, goin' out that girl house like so."

Amelia gently but firmly turned her mother toward the house. "Juju scared to death of that man," she said.

"He need to leave her be," Miss Evangeline said as they walked back into the house. "I tol' him that for true, me."

"He do what he do, Mama," Amelia said. "Nobody tell him nothin'."

She closed the front door behind them and led her mother down the hall toward the kitchen.

"Fifty-seven year," Miss Evangeline muttered. "I been raisin' him now fifty-seven year."

She inched along down the hallway, the tennis balls on her walker leaving snail trails of water on the hardwood floor.

Maggie straddled her tree limb, her arms around the trunk of the old oak, and tried not to think of dry clothes, or sunshine, or hot coffee.

She had no idea how long they'd been up in the tree. Thirty minutes? An hour? It felt like much more than that, though she knew it couldn't be. Her skin felt raw from the beating the rain was giving it.

She looked over at Kyle, squinting as the rain stabbed at her eyes. He was on another limb, a little bit higher than Maggie's, and he hugged the trunk as he leaned against it. She could see that he was shaking, and she felt the weight and substance of her failure to protect him.

"Mom!" she heard Sky yell, and Maggie looked at her daughter. Sky was looking toward the front yard, and Maggie turned to see. At first, Maggie wasn't sure what Sky was looking at, but then she realized that Boudreaux's huge truck was slowly moving toward them.

It was a good twenty yards away, but it looked like it might hit their tree. It wasn't moving very quickly, but it was a heavy truck, and they were in an old tree. Maggie yelled to be heard above the storm. "Hold on!"

Then she braced herself and waited for Boudreaux's truck to hit the tree.

⚓   ⚓   ⚓

Boudreaux didn't know he'd passed out until the water took him again and he woke up drowning.

He reached out his hands and felt the ground moving beneath him, felt mud and rocks and the roots of trees. He pulled his knees up under him, let the water drag his knees along the bumpy ground, and lifted his head up into the blessed air.

He was being carried through some woods, and he made out a few cypress and oaks as he passed them, heaving and coughing and leaving a trail of vomit behind him. He wasn't moving all that fast, but it was fast enough given his condition, and he considered just going with the flow until he hit the river, and letting it take him out to his beloved bay.

But then he remembered how upset Miss Evangeline would be with him, and how upset God already was, and he wasn't all that anxious to turn up dead before either one of them.

He paddled at the water with his arms, arms that felt like they'd been weighted down with chains, and tried to spot something to grab on to, but the water from the sky colluded with the water from the ground to blind and disorient him.

He tried to get his knees off the ground, to stop the beating they were getting from the rocks and roots beneath the surface, but the water wasn't all that deep and he wasn't all that buoyant. The best he could do was to keep them from dragging, but they still smacked against anything taller than a dandelion, and he wondered if he would soon have to contend with a broken kneecap in addition to his other immediate troubles.

Finally, he was pushed in the general direction of a large pile of debris, an assortment of brush, branches, a kid's bicycle, a broken pallet, and what looked like a chaise lounge, all hung up between two trees. He unexpectedly felt his knees come off the ground, and realized that he'd hit some kind of dip or trough, and he managed to get one foot and then the other underneath him.

He wasn't exactly walking, more being propelled, but he was able to use his feet to angle himself toward the debris pile. He grabbed onto the thin trunk of the nearest tree, and pulled his upper body up onto the pallet.

He threw up more water and the last of his chicory coffee, then rested there for a moment, his face pressed against the rough but comforting wood.

He blinked his eyes against the rain and looked at the woods he'd found himself in. He had no idea where he was. He wasn't even sure if he was still on Maggie's property. There were quite a few wooded areas along this section of the river.

It occurred to him then to wonder if this was where Maggie had been raped all those years ago, and the thought that it might be left him feeling more alone, yet suddenly surrounded by ghosts; ghosts of both the dead and of the living, as they had been twenty-two years ago.

The edge of the pallet was pressing uncomfortably against his torn abdomen, and he turned around so that his back was against the pallet, still gripping the wood with one shaky hand. He rested his head against the pallet, feeling more drained and weary than he could remember ever feeling before.

His eyes closed and he saw gentle morning waves flowing up onto the sand out on the island. Saw the sky lightening to a deep, bright pink and the seagulls hovering in the air in front of him. Saw Gregory standing there, pale as moonlight, with his ridiculous bag of bread, tossing out bits and pieces like he was on an early morning picnic.

"You've had your moment of peace, Gregory," he'd said to him quietly. "Let's get on with it."

Gregory looked over at him, one eye twitching, his Adam's apple bobbing as he swallowed once, hard. Boudreaux bobbed his .45 automatic at him, just once, to emphasize his desire to move it along, and Gregory stuffed the empty bread bag in his left pocket, then reached for the revolver tucked in the front of his waistband.

"You won't cock that thing and aim it before I've had time to blow the genitals right off your body. You understand that, do you not?" Boudreaux asked him.

Gregory only nodded, then slowly drew out the old .38. "Easy, son," Boudreaux cautioned. "Now put it in your mouth."

"Oh, geez," Gregory whispered.

"Do it now. Don't you get that thumb anywhere near that hammer until you've done so."

He watched Gregory turn the barrel toward himself, watched his hand shake uncontrollably as he slowly drew it toward his face. Then Gregory's legs started shaking.

"Oh, sit down, damn it," Boudreaux said, and Gregory practically fell to the sand.

Boudreaux stepped over to one side of him, his gun pointed between Gregory's legs. "Do it."

Gregory looked up at him helplessly. "I said I was sorry," he managed to say.

"I don't care that you're sorry," Boudreaux answered quietly.

"But I confessed...I told you of my own free will," Gregory said.

"And I appreciate that."

"Please, I told you I was leaving. For good."

"You also told me you'd considered suicide," Boudreaux answered. "And it's only because you're my nephew that you're being given the chance to do so."

He saw Gregory look down at the gun in his lap, could almost see him thinking.

"I can shoot you three times before you manage to raise that gun, son. But I won't. I'll blow a hole between your legs and then cut you into seventeen pieces while you're still bleeding to death, do you understand?"

Gregory nodded weakly, then shakily raised the .38.

"Both hands," Boudreaux told him, and Gregory awkwardly gripped the revolver in his two trembling hands and slowly brought it toward him.

"Please. I didn't know. I told you, I didn't know," he pleaded in a near-whisper.

"It doesn't matter what you knew," Boudreaux said calmly. "In your mouth"

He watched Gregory insert the muzzle into his mouth, saw a disgusting line of saliva drip from his lower lip as he did it.

"Point it up, moron."

Gregory tilted the muzzle upward toward the back of his head.

"Cock it."

Gregory's hands trembled violently as he stretched out a thumb and pulled the hammer back.

"If you make me shoot you, you will die slowly and painfully and without any mercy whatsoever. I know you believe this," Boudreaux said. "I know you know it to be true."

Gregory closed his eyes, and Boudreaux saw a tear spill from the corner of his right eye. He felt nothing because of it. There was only the cold, deep, unrelenting anger.

"Do it now," he repeated.

Gregory's finger twitched within the trigger guard. Boudreaux leaned a little closer, stretched his arm a little nearer to Gregory's manhood, careful not to put himself in front of Gregory.

"One...two...th—" he said, and the gunshot rang out, thumping Boudreaux's ears. He saw a spray of red from the back of Gregory's head before he looked away at the Gulf, heard a soft thump as Gregory's body fell backwards into the sand.

The gulls had risen into the air at the report, and Boudreaux had seen them in his peripheral vision as they landed once again. Then he'd flipped his safety back on, tucked the gun into the back of his waistband, and crossed himself before he'd headed back up to his car.

Boudreaux swiped weakly at his face, trying to clear away the rain and one solitary tear. He still felt that it had been assisted suicide more than anything else, and he still believed it had been the right and just thing to do. Yet he knew that at some point soon, probably that very day, God might want to discuss it with him.

⚓   ⚓   ⚓

There was nothing Maggie and the kids could do but watch, as the truck was pushed along the side of the house. Then, when it was about fifteen feet away, it began to turn counterclockwise. The bed of the truck slowly came around, and Maggie was expecting it to coast into them broadside, when the right front bumper or wheel well slammed into one of the house's concrete footings.

There was a loud, metallic groaning, and the bed of the truck kept sweeping slowly toward the tree, then stopped. They watched to see if the truck would break free from the pillar, but it didn't. Maggie could see now that the pillar had caught between the wheel well and the right front tire. After a moment, the screech of grinding metal stopped, and the water coursed under and around the truck.

Maggie stared at the truck. It sat tall on its oversized tires, and the roof of the cab was just five feet or so below the side deck of the house. If they could get up on top of the cab, they could climb up onto the deck.

She looked at the limbs of the old oak tree. A couple of the sturdier lower limbs of the tree reached within about six feet of the truck's bed. Theoretically, they could jump to it, but she had no way of telling if that would make the truck jerk free. They could also get down from the tree, make their way to the truck, and climb up into the bed, but they'd have to be on the ground behind it first, and that seemed far riskier. If the truck broke free, it would either coast over them or crush them against the tree.

Maggie watched the truck for a few minutes, trying so hard to detect the slightest movement that she began to imagine she saw it. But the truck got no closer, and she yelled at Sky.

"Sky!" Her daughter looked over at her. "I think we can get up to the deck from the truck."

Sky squinted her eyes against the rain to look at the truck, then looked back at Maggie. "It'll start moving again."

"Maybe. Maybe not," Maggie yelled back. "But we can't stay up here indefinitely."

Maggie slipped one foot down to the limb below her, then swung her other leg off of her branch.

"Mom! Let me go first," Sky yelled.

"No! I'll jump over there and we'll see what happens," Maggie yelled back. "If it holds, you come so I can get you up on the deck to help Kyle."

Holding on to the branch above her, Maggie inched her way out on the limb. It was slippery, and the rain seemed to be intentionally sweeping sideways into her face, but she eventually got out as far as she could before the limb thinned out too much to dependably hold her weight.

From where she stood, there was only about five feet of air between her and the bed of the truck. If she pushed off well enough, it was an easy jump to the back of the truck. She took a deep breath, and jumped.

She cleared the tailgate by a good twelve inches, but the bed was as slick as ice, and she went down onto her knees with a thump. She heard metal and concrete give a short chorus of complaint, but the truck held. She stood up carefully, feet planted wide, and waited for a moment before looking over at Sky, who was already making her way over to the other limb.

Maggie glanced up at Kyle, and felt a pressure in her chest at the wide-eyed look of fear on his face. She tried to give him a reassuring look, then turned her attention back to Sky. The girl was inching out on the slippery branch.

"Be careful, Sky, but push off as best you can," Maggie yelled, moving over to give Sky more room to land. The truck bounced a bit, but held.

Sky got out as far as she could, her hands gripping the branch above her, then looked over at her mother. Maggie nodded at her, and she took a deep breath and jumped, one leg out in front like she was jumping a hurdle.

Maggie's eyes closed involuntarily as Sky went airborne, then opened again as she felt her daughter's weight hit the bed of the truck. Sky slid, almost did a split, and nearly took Maggie down, but Maggie gripped the chrome side rail of the truck bed and held on.

They both remained motionless for a moment, as they listened to the short grind of metal up front. The truck might have slipped just a bit; Maggie wasn't sure. But it held. She looked over at Sky.

"Okay. I'm going to get over to the cab, then I'll help you get up on the roof," Maggie yelled. "It's gonna be slippery up there. Get hold of the deck rails as fast as you can."

Sky nodded, wiping the rain from her eyes, and Maggie made her way over to the cab, just behind the passenger seat, hanging onto the rail to keep from sliding. There was a slight incline to the truck that made it difficult to walk on the slick metal.

Once she was at the cab, Maggie hung onto the rail with her right hand, and turned and stretched her left hand out to Sky. "Come on," she yelled.

Sky reached out and grabbed her hand, and made her way over to the cab.

"Get one foot up on the front of the bed there, and one on this rail," Maggie yelled. "Then see if you can reach across the roof and grab that light rail over the windshield to help you get up there."

Sky did as she was told, using Maggie's hand to help steady her until she had both feet up on the frame of the truck bed. Maggie moved up against the back window of the cab so that she could hang on to Sky's hand while she got on all fours on the cab roof.

"I've got it!" Sky yelled back, and Maggie reluctantly let go of her hand, and watched Sky carefully rise up and grab onto the deck rails. Maggie was relieved to see that she'd misjudged the distance from the cab to the deck. Once Sky was standing, her knees were just below the deck.

Sky held onto the deck rail and climbed up, swung a leg over the top rail, then vaulted up onto the deck. The relief that Maggie felt, seeing her daughter back to the safety of the house, was almost overwhelming.

She turned and looked back at the tree, where Kyle was starting to make his way out onto the limb from which they had jumped.

"Kyle, that's far enough," Maggie yelled when he got to the point where the branch became too thin. "You can jump from there!"

Kyle looked over at the truck bed, then looked at her and nodded, though whether he was agreeing with her or reassuring himself, she wasn't sure.

He paused for just a moment, then kicked one leg out and jumped.

The truck shifted just a bit as he landed and fell to his knees, but it didn't pull loose. Maggie reached down and helped him up, still holding onto the side rail, and she steadied him as he made his way to the cab.

Sky was bent over the deck railing, one arm stretched toward the truck. Kyle held onto Maggie's hand as he got up on the edge of the truck bed, then climbed up onto the roof of the cab on his hands and knees. Maggie had to let him go so that he had his hands free, and she held her breath as he slid around a bit before reaching up and grabbing Sky's hand.

"Come on, Buddy," Sky yelled. "I got you."

Kyle finally reached up and snatched Sky's hand, and she held him as he grabbed onto the deck rail. Suddenly, the truck shifted just a bit, with the sound of metal against concrete, and Kyle's feet slipped out from under him. Maggie instinctively lunged for him over the roof of the cab, though she couldn't quite reach him.

He hung onto the rail, and Sky hung onto him, and after a moment, he got his feet back underneath him, put a foot up onto the deck and hauled himself over the rail. As his weight left the cab roof, the truck groaned again, and Maggie could feel it shifting.

Maggie couldn't reach the light bar from the bed of the truck, so she put a foot up on the side of the bed, and lunged across the roof for the light bar. She grabbed on, then pushed herself up to a crouch so that she could reach Sky's hand, just as she heard the metal screeching once more and the truck seemed to slide out from under her.

She reached out to grab the light bar once again, but the truck jerked and she fell backwards off of the roof and flat onto her back in the truck bed. Her head slammed against the floor of the bed, and just before she passed out, she heard Kyle yell for her and saw the deck slipping away.

FOURTEEN

O n what seemed like his 714th attempt, Wyatt got somebody's phone to ring. It was Dwight's, which had been going straight to voice mail all day.

"Hello?"

"Dwight, it's Wyatt."

"Oh hey, Wyatt," Dwight said, just a little bit louder than usual. "You had your surgery?"

"No, that's tomorrow," Wyatt answered. "What's going on over there with the hurricane?"

"Aw, hell, Wyatt, it's just one big mess," Dwight said. "All downtown's flooded. We got surges as high as seven feet. National Guard's been all over the place since late last night, evacuating people. Have you been talking to Vince?"

Vince was a thirty-year veteran, soon to retire, and was acting in Wyatt's stead during his surgery and recovery.

"No, I haven't been able to get hold of anydamnbody," Wyatt said.

"Yeah, phones are pretty spotty," Dwight said. "In and out, mostly out. What time's your surgery?"

"Don't worry about that, Dwight," Wyatt said shortly. "Have you seen or heard from Maggie?"

"Maggie? Well, no. I talked to her the other day. Why?"

"Well, she was supposed to be leaving early last night to pick her parents up in Jacksonville, but she's not there."

"You don't say. And you can't get her on the phone?"

Wyatt grimaced at Dwight. Even though the guy couldn't see him, it made Wyatt feel better. "Well, no, Dwight. I can't."

"Huh. Well, I haven't heard from her," Dwight said. "If she left early last night, though, she should be fine. It didn't start getting really bad here 'til real early this morning."

"If she was fine, she'd be answering her phone," Wyatt said. "In Jacksonville."

"Well, yeah, I see your point, Boss. I just don't know what to tell you. We've been running every which way all day, rescuing people that didn't evacuate, trying to shore up the sea wall, helping to board up some places better than they were. There's a whole lot of damage."

"Any loss of life?' Wyatt asked.

"Not that we know of yet."

"Well, is there any way you or somebody else can run out and check Maggie's house?" Wyatt asked. "Just in case."

"Heck, Boss, Bluff Road's a mess from about Waddell Road on out," Dwight said. "It's those bony ass pine trees. They're down all over the place. Weather guys say maybe we had a small tornado touch down, but we've been having gusts up to 50mph, and that could do it, too."

Wyatt sighed. "Have they started clearing it any?"

"Not yet, Wyatt. We've pretty much got every hand full right here in town. There's been some flooding here and there out Maggie's way, off the creeks, but nothing her house couldn't handle. Maybe she just got a later start than she thought and couldn't get out."

"Yeah."

"I get that you're worried, Boss, I do."

"Yeah." Dwight was one of the few people, as far as Wyatt knew, who knew that he and Maggie had some kind of a relationship. "I hear 98's pretty much washed out everywhere. What's the bridge look like?"

"Uh, it's semi-serviceable, but they're not letting anybody cross it," Dwight said. "Why?"

"'Cause I'm about fifty miles out."

"Well crap, Wyatt. Uh, what about Orlando?"

"It's still where it was," Wyatt answered. "Who's not letting people cross it? The Guard?"

"Yeah. But what about your surgery?"

"Get with somebody over there, ask them not to give me any crap, 'cause I'm driving into Apalach."

"Uh...will do, Boss. If I can get to somebody," Dwight said. "I'm over here at the airport right now, helping with the shelter."

"Just see what you can do, okay?"

"Okee-doke," Dwight said, and Wyatt hung up before Dwight could make him feel like an idiot again for ducking out on the surgery to check on Maggie.

Freaking Maggie, with her boondocks, her developmentally-disabled chickens, and her pet serial killer.

⚓ ⚓ ⚓

Boudreaux took in a mouthful of rain and swished it around before trying to lean over and spit it out. What he managed to do was more or less dribble it down his shirt, and this annoyed him, despite the shirt being torn, bloodied, and soaking wet.

His left arm ached from the strain of hanging onto the pallet, and he shifted himself over a bit and changed to his right arm. It concerned him just a little that his abdomen didn't seem to hurt as much as he thought it probably should. When he looked down, he could see swirls of fresh blood leaving his body and joining the rush to the river. It seemed to be less blood than before, but still a troublesome amount.

He leaned back against the pallet, which was a lot easier than trying to stay upright, and closed his eyes for a moment. He'd never felt his age before, but he was feeling it now. He was exhausted, cold, and thirsty. He opened his mouth to get some more rain, held it for a moment, then swallowed and opened his eyes.

It took him a moment to understand what he was seeing. His truck was about fifty feet away, headed more or less straight for him. It was moving slowly, but in a fairly determined fashion.

At first, he thought that Maggie was coming to get him, but then he realized that he didn't hear the monstrous diesel engine. When he looked up toward the windshield, he saw that Maggie wasn't driving. No one was.

He'd survived driving through a hurricane, tussling with some idiot, getting slashed, and nearly drowning. Now God was going to run him over with his own truck. As he lifted his free arm to cross himself, it occurred to him that he was having an unusually ironic day.

⚓   ⚓   ⚓

Sky and Kyle had stood on the deck for more than a few minutes after the truck had disappeared from view. It was almost as though they expected the truck to somehow return, with their mother at the wheel. Sky was crazily reminded of an old country song her Dad used to sing, something about giving him enough acres and he could turn the truck around. She allowed herself about half a second to wish he was there now, then forced herself to think.

"Kyle, come on!" she said quickly, and ran for the front door with Kyle on her heels.

"What about Mom?" he yelled.

"This *is* about Mom."

She opened the door, which was nearly ripped out of her hands by the wind, sidestepped a very concerned Coco, but then slid through the puddle on the floor. There was a momentary confluence of pedestrian and poultry, then she ran toward the hall and Stoopid flailed into the living room before he could be trod upon by Kyle.

Sky ran into her room and threw open her closet, tossed aside a couple of boxes and backpacks, and grabbed up the pile of rope in the back.

"The fire ladder?" Kyle asked over her shoulder.

"I should have thought of it when I first got back up on the deck," Sky said, walking quickly back down the hall. "Stupid. You and Mom wouldn't have had to climb up that freakin' truck."

"What if she doesn't come back?" Kyle asked as he followed her back into the main room.

"What do you mean, dude? She's coming back."

"I don't think she was awake."

"She will be," Sky said and she opened the door, pushing Coco back with her foot. "No, Coco, stay."

She turned around and looked at Kyle as the rain stabbed at her back. "You stay, too."

"What? No!"

"She will freaking kill me if I let you stand out on that deck and get whomped by somebody's yard flamingo or something," Sky said. "I'm serious. Stay in here. Feed Coco and find something for Stoopid. Some salad or Nyquil or something."

She went back out onto the deck, only realizing afterwards that she should have grabbed a coat or something out of her closet. She went back to the rail of the side deck, and was about to hook the rope fire ladder to the rail when she decided that the wind would probably bork it up, so she set it down by her feet and waited, arms wrapped around herself as though they would keep her dry or warm or calm.

At least she could put her back mostly to the wind and the rain, and still be able to watch for her mother to come back. And she would come back. They might have their differences sometimes, but Sky knew her mother. If she had arms and legs, she'd come back for her kids.

⚓ ⚓ ⚓

Maggie felt the needles of rain stabbing into the skin of her face and chest, and she turned on her side and curled into a fetal position, with one arm over her head.

The back of her head was throbbing, and she wondered vaguely if a person could have more than one concussion at a time, or if the original one just got worse. Either way, the pain and pressure in her neck, her face, and the back of her head were starting to wear on her, and the slightest movement made fireworks go off behind her eyes.

She opened them anyway, and saw that she was in one of the back corners of the truck bed, up against the tailgate. Something about that seemed odd to her, until she braved movement and looked at the tops of the trees she could see, and at the sky.

The truck was tilted to the side, and she was piled in the lower back corner. She tried to think what the truck could be tilted on, without having to sit up and look over the side. There were a few spots in these woods where erosion had caused the trees to tug up on their roots, which led to more erosion and the creation of some gulleys and dips.

She looked around the truck without moving, but saw nothing she could use to cover her head. The bed was completely empty.

The rain was relentless, and she just needed to be out of it for a moment. She pulled up the bottom of her T-shirt and managed to stretch it enough to cover her face. It was soaked, but it lessened the impact of the raindrops and made her feel like she had some respite.

The throbbing in her head increased in intensity, and she wished she could form words to pray, but the only word that came to mind was "stop." She just needed it to stop.

She laid there, curled up in a ball, for what she thought was maybe a few minutes, but could have been an hour, and was about to try to sit up when she heard a groaning, felt a shifting of her present world, and the truck flipped onto its back before she realized that it was happening.

She fell face first into the water, and then the truck came down on top of her with a tremendous splash.

When the truck had glided past Boudreaux, skirting him by more than six feet, he'd leaned back and taken several deep, wet breaths. The debris pile didn't allow him to see behind him, but he waited to hear the truck hit a tree, and was surprised when he never did, though the trees were fairly well-spaced out here in this section of the woods. He never heard the truck hit anything, and for all he knew, it was continuing on down to the river, which could be fifty yards or half a mile behind him.

He was disoriented and in an unfamiliar place, and he would have had no idea where the river was in relation to him if it weren't for the flow of the flood waters. The sun was nowhere to be found, and the sky was an unbroken sheet of titanium gray that offered no clue to his current place in the world.

He was entirely unaccustomed to this lack of control over his present and future, but he supposed on reflection that he had been ceding at least some control for months now. Ever since the night that Gregory had told him what he'd done, thinking it would spur Boudreaux to throw money at him and make him go away.

He had now spent the last two months carefully cultivating a relationship with Maggie, slowly building her interest and her trust, delicately revealing himself to her at an annoyingly but entirely necessary slow pace, and now it was likely to all be for naught.

He was going to bleed to death out here in somebody's back yard, and all of that planning and all of that patience would amount to nothing in the end. He shouldn't have wasted the last few weeks, but he hadn't known what to say to her after she'd shot Patrick, so he'd just avoided her altogether.

What should he have said? *I'm terribly sorry that my nephew raped you twenty years ago and that my stepson had your husband killed last month, but I'm very sincere in my desire to continue building this relationship between us*?

He'd spent the last two weeks trying to decide the best way to approach Maggie again, to get past Gregory and Patrick and finally introduce her to the truth in a way that would put her niggling suspicions to rest and yet wouldn't make her loathe him.

He should have thought a little faster and made a decision a little sooner, because it looked like the last two months were shortly to become moot.

He looked down and gently fingered his torn midsection, which was still releasing blood into the water in artful little feathers, then he dropped his head back against the pallet.

He supposed that, in the end, it was just as well. She already had a father, one she loved deeply, and Boudreaux had to admit that Gray had done a better job of raising another man's child than he himself had.

CHAPTER

FIFTEEN

G ray Redmond drummed his fingers on the table as he watched the TV that hung over the bar. With no-where really to go, he and Georgia had dragged their small suitcases from the port to the nearest chain ho-tel, where the desk clerk had been kind enough to stow them in back until they figured out if they needed a room. People in the more urban parts of Florida weren't always the most pleasant, but most people tended to become more helpful during a hurricane, even if the storm wasn't local.

Gray watched the same footage of the same scenes that the news had been showing for the last couple of hours, and the obligatory live shots of excited reporters in wind-breakers, tilting against the wind and rain as they mar-veled over the gusts, the damage, the surges. The weath-er people were always so happy when a good storm hit; it could be a real career-maker.

According to the latest news, Faye seemed to have de-cided not to make landfall after all. After twenty-four hours of beating the coastline from Cedar Key on up to Pensaco-la, she was turning northwest and looking to make her way

over to Louisiana. The experts predicted she'd hit somewhere between Biloxi and Baton Rouge sometime early in
the evening. Meanwhile, the southernmost bands of wind
and rain were still giving the Panhandle grief, but in smaller quantities.

Gray watched as they ran footage from early that morning, of the storm surge on Saint George Island and near
downtown Apalach. There had been no film of the flooding further inland, caused by the incredible amount of rain
that had been dumped into the river and the many creeks
that threaded through the area. But Gray didn't need to see
it to know that Maggie and the kids were in a bad spot if
they were still at home.

"If you were still oystering full time, I think I'd lay down
and cry right now," Georgia said quietly.

Gray looked over at her and noted the way worry was
tugging at the skin beneath her beautiful eyes. "It's bad.
But we've been through worse," he said.

The strength of the storm itself had done its own damage, but the incredible amount of rain being dumped into
the bay would have its own effect. Part of the reason Apalachicola oysters were among the best in the world was the
delicate balance of fresh to salt water found where the river opened into the Gulf.

One of the threats to the oysters in recent years had
been Atlanta's insistence on taking water from the river to
fill its swimming pools, creating an increase in the bay's sa-
linity. But too much fresh water created the same problem
from the other direction. The last time they'd had a really good storm, it had taken almost three years for the oysters to bounce back.

"I just hate to see it," Georgia said. "The oystermen can
never get a good break for very long."

Gray nodded, understanding that focusing on the plight of the oystermen and their families was a lot easier for her than focusing on the whereabouts and well-being of her daughter and grandchildren. Georgia was not weak by any means, but sometimes she found strength in distraction. Gray lacked that skill.

He dialed Boudreaux's number for the seventh time since they'd spoken, and again it went straight to voice mail. He didn't bother leaving another one. He slapped the phone shut and ran a hand through his slightly long, light brown hair. Then he stretched out one long, lanky leg and stood up from the stool.

"Let's go, Georgia," he said.

She looked up at him. "Go where?" she asked.

"Home."

He tossed a few bills down on the bar to pay for their tea, and shoved his cell phone in his shirt pocket. "We'll walk back to the port and rent a car."

"But Wyatt said we should stay here," she said, though she stood.

"Maggie's not coming here, baby, and I'm not going to sit here pretending she might," Gray said quietly. "I'm going to go home and find out what's going on with our girl."

⚓ ⚓ ⚓

Maggie had fully expected the truck to crush her, and it took a moment for it to register in her mind that the truck had rolled over her, but not onto her.

She lifted her head from the water and got her feet under her, but when she tried to stand, she banged her head on the truck bed. The water was about four feet deep, and she only had about six inches of clearance above it.

It took her a moment to get oriented. There was little light, but by moving her palms around the truck bed she discovered that the truck was still on a slant. The other side of the bed was completely under water.

She moved back over to the other side and stayed in her semi-squat for a moment, breathing deeply of the air there and trying to focus. Then she moved back to the tailgate, to the side that was above the water. She felt around with her left boot, and could feel the small slope of ground that the truck was leaning against. She then tried to gauge how much space there was for her to swim out, but what her foot told her didn't seem to enlighten her much. She took a breath and squatted down.

The way the truck was leaning against the slope, she had a wedge-shaped opening to get through. It looked like it would be tight, but it was definitely large enough. She straightened up a bit and took a couple of breaths, then went back under and straightened her legs out behind her.

Her upper half cleared the wedge-shaped opening just fine, but as she passed through, she felt a jerk at her waist and was stopped cold. She got a foot under her and tried to push through, but she was hung up.

She reached around behind her and found that one of the belt loops on the back of her shorts was caught on something at the corner of the tailgate. She tugged at it, but wasn't able to tear it free, and she felt panic starting to assert itself in her chest. She wasn't close enough to the surface of the water to be able to curve upward and get a breath of air, and when she tried to back up under the truck bed, she couldn't do that, either.

Her animal instinct wanted to thrash around and tear at the shorts, but she forced herself to move more deliberately, reserving oxygen in her muscles and avoiding full on panic. She reached around back one more time to try to work her shorts free, but quickly saw that she was wasting time by trying to free something she couldn't see.

She grabbed at her belt buckle and quickly undid it, then started to pull herself out of her shorts. She got far enough to break the surface of the water and take a gulp of air, then gasped as one of her boots refused to clear the leg of her shorts. She kicked and pushed at it with her free boot, but finally had to curl up back underneath the water and push the hiking boot off of her foot.

She surfaced again, reached overhead to slap the boot up on the underside of the truck, then submerged again and wrested her shorts from the corner of the tailgate and pushed herself back up to the surface. She grabbed onto the truck and stood, and when she did she saw the body.

It was Dewitt Alessi, with one arm bending in entirely the wrong direction and wrapped around the front axle. He was on his back, more or less. A gaping, almost bloodless slice from one side of his neck to the other looked like some kind of macabre smile but, judging by the expression on his face, he hadn't been very cheerful at the end.

Maggie made herself turn away. Boot in one hand and shorts in the other, she scrambled over the two foot incline and pushed herself over to a large holly bush.

She looped an arm around one of its thicker branches and went through a laborious process of turning her sodden shorts right side out while she gripped her boot between her knees, then pulling her shorts back on, and sliding her boot back onto her foot one-handed.

The boots were common sense; the last thing she needed was to slice up her feet on some kind of debris. The shorts...well, dead or alive, she wasn't going to be found in her freaking underwear.

The task was surprisingly wearying, owing much to the fact that she was waist-deep in moving water, and she hung onto the holly bush for a few minutes afterward, getting her breath and her bearings.

She had a rough idea where she was, judging herself to be in the woods at the back of the Grahams' property, just downriver from her own. The easiest thing to do, physically, would be to go with the flow of the water and hope that she came out somewhere near their dock, where she knew they kept a small aluminum flat-bottom. But that was a big hope. She could come out even just five feet down river of the dock and be screwed. Or, she could hit the dock head on and find out the boat was gone.

She looked back at the woods and sighed wearily. She was going to have to fight the water all the way back to the house. If she was right about her general location, it meant a good quarter of a mile. Nothing to it on dry land, but a bit of a trek as things were. On the positive side, the rain had let up noticeably and the flow of the water seemed to have slowed.

Maggie took a few deep breaths to gather her resolve, and started wading against the current in what she assumed was the general direction of her house.

⚓ ⚓ ⚓

Wyatt coasted to a stop in front of the yellow traffic barriers that had been lined up across 98, a good fifty yards before the bridge. Two National Guard trucks sat on the side of the road, and a few Guardsmen in military-issue rain ponchos stood on the swale. One of them approached Wyatt's rental car, and Wyatt rolled down his window.

"Sir, the bridge isn't passable. You'll need to turn around."

The guy was young, maybe in his early twenties, with white blond hair and dimples his mother probably doted on.

"Not passable, or not advisable?" Wyatt asked, as he lifted his butt enough to fish out his ID.

"Sir, the bridge isn't safe at this time and we're not allowing anyone to pass."

"Well, I can understand that, but I'm the sheriff of this county and I'm heading into Apalach," Wyatt said as he flipped open his badge case.

The soldier looked at Wyatt's ID and looked back up at him. "I see, sir. However, the bridge isn't safe to travel."

"Is it washed out?"

"Not necessarily, no, but it's got some surge damage," the soldier answered. "We've got trucks on the way with sandbags to shore up the retaining walls, but it's basically underwater at the Apalachicola end, there where it meets that little island."

"The fill," Wyatt said.

"The what, sir?"

"The fill. We call that little piece of land there 'the fill' because they used dirt from the landfill to make it."

"I see. Yeah, well, it's currently underwater."

"How much water?"

The young soldier thought about that for a moment. "I can't say exactly, sir, but enough that your car's unlikely to make it off the bridge. I don't advise you attempt it."

"Well, while I appreciate your advice, I'm going to have to ignore it," Wyatt said politely. "Now, are you authorized to shoot me or anything if I just keep going?"

"Well, no sir, just to detain."

"Are you going to attempt to detain the Sheriff of Franklin County for responding to a state of emergency?"

"Uh…" The soldier looked around, probably hoping to find someone more enthused about answering that question.

"I need you to move that barrier for me, okay?"

"Sir, I really need to speak with someone—"

"You're speaking with me, son, and I'd prefer that you move that barrier for me *before* I proceed. But I am proceeding."

"Uh…yes, sir."

Wyatt felt a little sorry for the kid as he watched him run over and pull one of the barriers aside. He was probably just trying to earn some college tuition, and he was unlikely to be having a great deal of fun out here in the storm. Nevertheless, Wyatt needed to get to town.

He put the car back in drive and pulled through the barriers, then slowly eased onto the bridge. Normally, there was quite a nice view of the bay from the roughly five-mile crossing, but today visibility was minimal. Although the rain had calmed somewhat, it was still there, and all Wyatt could see was choppy water on either side.

A strong gust made the rental car shimmy, and Wyatt slowed from twenty miles an hour down to fifteen. He sighed. He could be relaxing in a nice dry hotel bed, watching ESPN and ordering room service cheeseburgers.

Instead, he was driving through a hurricane across a screwed up bridge, and doing it in a freaking Ford Focus, no less.

⚓ ⚓ ⚓

Sky had eventually had to come in out of the storm. The wind and rain were too much, and the occasional debris was a hazard. Before she did go in, she grabbed the cordless drill from the toolbox and removed the plywood from one of the living room windows. Mom would be pissed if the window broke, but Sky could deal with pissed. What she couldn't deal with was watching for her mother from the deck.

After she dragged Coco out onto the deck and finally convinced her to pee there, Sky and Kyle both changed into dry clothes and took up a post on the window seat, where they had a fairly good vantage point to watch for their mother's safe return.

Stoopid was on the kitchen floor, talking to himself while he tucked into a plate of what Kyle called "cantaloupe intestines." If Stoopid's enthusiasm was any indication, these were apparently God's greatest invention since the hen.

The power was still out, so the stove clock was no help, but Sky figured they'd been sitting there for almost an hour.

"What if the truck went into the river?' Kyle asked after several minutes of silence.

"It didn't."

"How do you know?"

"Because there's too much crap between here and there," Sky said quietly. "Something stopped it eventually."

"What if it didn't?"

"It did," Sky said, unable to stop the annoyance from creeping into her voice.

She glanced over at Kyle and felt badly; he was a kid and he was scared, and he'd been given plenty of reasons to *be* scared.

"Look, dude," she said more kindly. "In a couple of days, everything will go back to sucking in a more general way. You'll be over at Thing 2's house killing your brain cells with Minecraft and I'll be nodding politely at Mom while she suggests that I might try listening to Clint Black or some kind of crap, and everything'll be cool. Okay?"

Kyle looked at her and sighed, then gave her a nod.

"Okay," Sky answered herself.

⚓ ⚓ ⚓

Maggie's legs were already trembling with exhaustion, and she hadn't made as much progress as she thought she should have, given the effort she'd expended. She was also incredibly thirsty, but she'd thrown up the few mouthfuls of rain she'd tried to take in, and she figured that this, along with some dizziness and confusion, pretty much confirmed her suspicion that she had a decent concussion. Either that, or she no longer cared for rain.

The water was definitely moving more slowly, which was helpful, but it was still waist deep, which was less so. Maggie was grateful, though, that the wind had died down a bit and the rain wasn't quite so torrential. Even so, she was fairly well convinced that she would never be dry or warm again.

She slogged over to a spindly pine and grabbed on, then leaned against it and took a few slow breaths. She thought then that if a bed had floated by, she'd have climbed on and pulled the wet covers over her head. The last time she was this tired, she'd been in the maternity ward at the hospital, listening to Kyle's first wails.

She waited a few minutes, then forced herself to push away from the tree and continue making her way toward the house. She'd gone about fifty feet when she stopped to grab onto another small tree, and glanced over at a pile of junk that had collected about fifty yards to her left.

Something too bright caught her eye, and she squinted at it through the rain, then wiped her eyes and looked again. White. It was Boudreaux's white shirt, though what she could see of the lower portion of it was red. His back, arm and head were on the junk pile and out of the water, but the rest of him was submerged. He wasn't moving, but she hadn't expected him to be moving the next time she saw him.

She changed direction, and started working her way diagonally toward him.

CHAPTER

SIXTEEN

A s Maggie neared the pile of debris, Boudreaux's eyes fluttered open, much to her amazement. He blinked up at the sky for a moment, then looked over at her. He seemed a little surprised to see her, too.

She waded over to the pile as he watched her come toward him, his normally deeply-tanned face alarmingly pale.

"Mr. Boudreaux," she said when she'd gotten there, like she'd just run into him at the library.

He nodded at her once. "Maggie," he answered, like he'd asked her to meet him at the library.

The water wanted to force Maggie back the way she'd worked so hard to come, so she pushed over to the pile of debris and let the water pin her there. She grabbed on to the pallet Boudreaux was leaning on, and looked at him.

Her face was only about ten inches from his, and she thought about the only other time she'd been that close to him physically, the night early on in their odd relationship when she had danced with him at the Cajun Festival. He'd looked great then; he didn't look so hot now.

"What are you doing out here?" he asked her weakly.

"I was checking out your truck," she said, trying to smile but primarily failing.

He blinked at her a few times. "What did you think?"

"It's a little rough," she answered.

He tried to smile too, and he too pretty much failed at it. Then he looked at her for a moment. "Where are your children?"

"In the house," she said. "I didn't quite make it."

"How far are we from the house?"

Maggie blew out a breath and looked off in the general direction she'd been heading. "Not that far, if we were out for a walk. Maybe three or four hundred yards past that clump of old cypress over there. My property line is just past them."

He looked where she was pointing, at a stand of trees and stumps about fifty yards away, then looked back at her. "It's amazing how weighty water is when it's moving against you, isn't it?"

She looked down at the water in front of him, saw tendrils of red slipping away from his midsection beneath the surface. When she looked up again, he was watching her.

"Please excuse me for saying it, but you don't look much better," he said.

She nodded and looked back down at his midsection.

"Did he hit you?"

Maggie thought it was an odd question, given that Boudreaux had burst in while Alessi was strangling her. "No, I fell on the stairs."

"Who was he?"

Maggie looked back up at him. "Richard Alessi's father."

Boudreaux nodded and his eyes drifted closed.

"Why did you come here, Mr. Boudreaux?"

He opened his eyes again and stared at her for a moment. "Your father was worried about you."

"But why would he call you?"

He seemed to consider his words before he answered. "Everybody knows I never evacuate."

Maggie was about to tell him that she didn't think he'd actually answered her question, but she felt a sudden lurching in her stomach, and she turned her back to him. She leaned over, but nothing came up. There was just an overwhelming nausea that rippled outward from her stomach to her follicles, and the fine hairs on her arms stood up in protest.

She closed her eyes and waited a moment until it subsided a bit, then she turned and laid her face against the rough wood of the pallet. When she opened her eyes, Boudreaux's were right there, staring back at her. Those impossibly blue eyes.

"What was the name of that song we danced to at the festival?" she asked him. "The one you said was your favorite?"

He frowned at her for a second, seeming surprised by the question. "*La Chanson de Mardi Gras*," he said. "The dance of Mardi Gras."

"It sticks with you."

"Yes."

Maggie felt her eyes drifting closed. "My mother wasn't too happy about me dancing with you that night," she said softly, and one corner of her mouth turned up in a smile.

"I can imagine," she heard him say after a moment.

Gray and Georgia had been on I-10 for more than an hour, the last half of it in silence as they each occupied themselves with their own thoughts. According to the radio, things were calming down in the Panhandle, but Gray hadn't been able to get through to Wyatt's number.

"I wish you hadn't called him," Georgia said when she finally broke their silence.

Gray cut his eyes at her.

"What I mean is, I wish you hadn't needed to," she added almost apologetically, then looked back out her window.

"So do I." He pinched at the bridge of his nose, his eyes feeling strained and tired. "But I knew he'd go."

She was quiet again for a moment, as she stared out at nothing.

"Why do you suppose that is?' she asked finally. "He's kept his word, left her alone all these years."

Gray chose his words carefully before he spoke. "Maggie thinks he feels guilty about what happened. That it was his nephew who did it."

Georgia looked over at her husband. "Why did he know, and we didn't?"

"The nephew told him, right before he killed himself." He looked over at her. "Maggie told me that."

Georgia looked back out the window and was quiet again for a moment. "What do you think?"

"I think it's a father's guilt." He caught his wife's skeptical look. "You think Gregory Boudreaux would have dared lay a hand on her if he'd known who she was? You think *anybody* would? But I think he's actually come to care for her, in whatever way he does that."

Georgia swallowed, then looked away. "We're going to have to talk to her, Gray, and she's going to despise me."

Gray sighed. "I'm not sure that we are, and no she won't. We were just kids. It was one night. We got through it, and she would, too."

They fell silent again for a moment, each with their own dread about having to dredge up the past, each with their own fear about the future.

"Let's just deal with right now," Gray said after a few minutes. "Let's just get home."

⚓ ⚓ ⚓

The boy soldier with the cute dimples had been right; the fill was mostly underwater.

The fill was a spit of land that sat at pretty much sea level, and connected the Apalachicola Bay bridge to the shorter John Gorrie Bridge, which went into downtown Apalach. Wyatt made it across the fill by what could only be called extended hydroplaning, with periodic episodes of actual driving.

Things got better for Wyatt as he finally made it to the John Gorrie, which gradually rose up out of the water and carried him across the Apalachicola River where it opened into the bay. Wyatt breathed a little bit better as he enjoyed the feeling of rubber actually meeting the road, until the bridge curved and descended into town.

Wyatt could see on either side of the bridge that downtown was flooded. He got the impression of descending into a watery ghost town, like Atlantis in the early stages of disappearing. There was no one out on the streets. The only cars were those that had been abandoned or parked in unfortunate locations.

Once Wyatt's car reached the street, he slowed to a crawl, and managed to coast for about a block in two feet of water before the Focus crapped out on him. He drifted more or less to the curb, turned off the ignition, set the parking brake just in case, and slowly opened his door.

Water flowed in and soaked the floorboards, and Wyatt wondered briefly if his insurance was going to cover it, then he carefully swung his legs into the water, feeling the protest from his left hip. He reached over and grabbed his cane, then took his time standing up, one hand on the cane and the other on the door.

Once he decided he was as steady as he was going to get, he slowly made his way over to the sidewalk and stepped up onto it. Then he started making his way up the street, hoping that he ran into the National Guard again before he either fell or passed out from the pain.

He was six-foot-four and the Sheriff of this freakin' county, and it would be embarrassing as hell to drown on the sidewalk.

⚓   ⚓   ⚓

"Maggie."

Boudreaux watched as Maggie's eyes moved behind her lids. He wasn't sure how long she'd been out; he might have drifted off for a few minutes as well. But before she'd lost consciousness, she'd been acting confused, had said something about the way the light reflected on the bay, and then wondered aloud how long a rooster could go without grit.

He didn't know if it was shock or perhaps a head injury, but she wasn't okay. He wasn't okay, either; in fact, he was surprised to still be breathing. But if he died shortly, she'd be out here alone and not thinking clearly. It was time to go.

"Maggie," he said again, almost yelling.

Her eyes fluttered open and blinked a few times against the rain, which was falling more gently, but still falling.

"Crap," she said quietly.

"We need to get you back to the house."

Maggie lifted her head and looked at him. "You can't. The more you move, the more you'll bleed."

"Then you go."

"No. I'm not leaving you out here."

"You're not staying."

"Someone will find us soon."

"Who? Coco?" he asked sharply. "Nobody's coming, Maggie."

"My Dad will," Maggie said. "He's not sitting around in Jacksonville. I promise you my father is already riding to the rescue."

Boudreaux felt a weight inside his chest as he watched her head drift back down to the pallet, saw her eyes shut. He blinked a couple of times as his eyes became warm and full, then he swallowed hard and slid his upper body off of the pallet, wincing as his abdomen seemed to come apart.

He splashed a handful of water into her face and she opened her eyes and threw up a hand to smack his away.

"I'm going to your house now," he said as he grabbed her wrist and pulled her with him. "And I would appreciate it if you'd come with me in case I need someone to carry my intestines."

CHAPTER
SEVENTEEN

W yatt thought someone was coming up behind him on a little scooter, which would have been odd, but when he turned around, he saw Axel Black-well pulling up alongside him in a little aluminum flat-bottom.

Axel, a shrimper friend of Maggie's from way back who was considered one of the local "hotties," was wearing a Boss Oyster baseball cap and smiling around a cigarette, looking for all the world like he was out after some catfish.

"Hey, Tripod, how's it going?" he asked Wyatt.

Wyatt stopped and gave Axel a look. "Dandy, Axel. How are things with you?"

"Not too bad," Axel answered. "Can I give you a lift somewhere?"

"I need to get out to Bluff Road."

Axel tossed his cigarette butt into the water. "Bluff Road is screwed up, man. Trees down everywhere."

"I heard. But I need to get out there."

"Why?"

"Nobody's heard from Maggie."

"Nobody's heard from anybody, Wyatt. Phone service sucks."

"Yeah, well, she was supposed to be in Jacksonville yesterday."

Axel squinted at Wyatt as he pulled a cigarette out of the pack in his flannel shirt and lit it. "That's different," he said, blowing out of plume of smoke.

"Think you can take me to some National Guard guys so they can run me out there?"

"Man, they're all over the place. But they're not getting out to Maggie's in those old cargo trucks." Axel stuck the cigarette between his teeth and took another drag. "I got something that'll get us there, though. See if you can climb in without tipping us the hell over."

Wyatt sighed and made his way over to the little boat. It didn't actually look like it would hold the both of them, but he didn't have any other ideas, and he needed to get out there to Maggie and the kids.

⚓   ⚓   ⚓

Sky and Kyle sat on the window seat, staring out the window at the flooded yard, and eating slices of bread from the bag.

"What time do you think it is?" Kyle asked.

"I don't know. With no sun, it's hard to tell," Sky answered, and handed her crust to Coco, who was sitting with her head draped onto the window seat.

"How long do you think she's been gone?"

Sky swallowed, not really wanting to answer. "I'm not sure, dude. Maybe a couple of hours?"

"I think it's more."

"I said I don't know, Kyle," Sky said, snapping without meaning to.

"Sorry," Kyle said quietly.

Sky sighed. "Me, too."

He was quiet for a moment, and when he spoke again, he didn't look at her. "I wish Dad was here."

Sky blinked a few times as her eyes watered. "Yeah."

"He could figure out what to do."

"Mom's smart, too, Kyle. And she's tough."

"I know."

They were silent again for a few minutes.

"You know, you look so much like him," Sky said finally. "Sometimes, when I look at you, it makes me feel better."

He looked over at her, and after a moment, he nodded. "That's cool."

Sky was uncomfortable with intimacy and "sappy stuff," so she looked away and distracted herself by watching Stoopid as he pulled at a thread from the little hole he'd dug in the corner of the loveseat.

Kyle followed her gaze. "She's gonna be kind of pissed about that, I bet."

"Duct tape," Sky answered.

⚓ ⚓ ⚓

Maggie slogged along just behind Boudreaux, feeling like her lungs and her legs were competing to see which one would give out first. She didn't know how Boudreaux was doing it.

Every now and then, she looked down into the water, and saw thin tendrils of blood swirling toward her, then separating and passing her on either side. She was wading in his bloody wake, and even though it wasn't a lot of blood compared to earlier, she didn't know how he still had some left.

They finally got past the dense clump of trees that marked her property line, and Maggie let out a deep breath as she realized that she was back on her own land. It didn't look like home, but it was. The vegetation was much thicker here and she couldn't see the house yet, but she knew it was there.

She looked over at Boudreaux. He was a good five inches or so taller than she was, and the water didn't come quite up to his waist, and she was glad that she was slightly behind him. She'd stolen one glance at his midsection earlier, had glimpsed a ragged tear and very pale, puffy flesh within it that should not have been visible to her. It had scared the crap out of her.

She looked at him now, saw the flash of his gold watch as he swung his arms over the water, and thought how odd it was to see him looking anything less than immaculate. He'd always exuded such a relaxed elegance. She thought, too, about the way he'd looked at the Cajun festival, just a couple of months ago, handsome and fit and full of energy, like a man twenty years his junior. It made her sad, somehow, to wonder if she'd see him dancing there next summer.

⚓ ⚓ ⚓

Wyatt gaped as Axel slid open the huge doors, letting more water spill into a building at Scipio Creek Marina that was normally used to house boats.

The pickup truck itself looked like a neon blue cake topper, perched on tires that probably came up to Wyatt's chest.

He looked over at Axel, who was grinning around the hind end of yet another cigarette.

"What the hell do you have this for?" Wyatt asked him.

"Mud racing, man." Axel pulled a set of keys out of his back pocket. "I got a vehicle for every situation."

"I don't doubt that," Wyatt said, as he hobbled toward the thing.

"Lemme grab you a step stool, man."

"I haven't needed a step stool since I was seven," Wyatt snapped.

"You do today, peg leg."

⚓ ⚓ ⚓

William the florist stood on the balcony of his and Robert's apartment, on the second floor of one of Apalach's many Victorians. He lit his cigarette and took a grateful drag of both it and the fresh air.

He loved Robert dearly, but after twenty-six years, he really could only handle so much togetherness in a space with boarded-up windows. The only light they'd had was from the French door to the balcony, which only remained uncovered because Robert didn't allow smoking in the house, and William wouldn't make it twenty-four hours without throwing Robert down the stairs if he was forced to go without. He'd rather replace a door than a lifelong partner, so there it was.

The rain had all but quit and, although there was still no sun, the sky had lightened to a sickly gray rather than a threatening one. This thing was almost over, and all they would have to contend with was a foot or two of water in the flower shop and a bunch of slippery insurance agents.

He heard a rumbling noise, an engine, and expected to see one of those hideously outdated Army trucks when he leaned over the rail to look down the street. Instead, he saw an apparition.

"Robert!" he called through the open door. "Come look at this nonsense."

Robert stepped out from the living room. "What?"

"That," William said, pointing with his cigarette.

Robert stepped over to the rail and looked at the bright blue truck headed their way, leaving a wake behind it that sent waves to either side of the street. "Oh, for Pete's sake."

"Look at these idiots," William said. "Just hanging out like the place isn't flooded. Like we're not having a hurricane, thank you."

"We're still here."

"We're still here because we're not going to some Hampton Inn in Tallahassee where they only pretend to change the sheets," William said. "We're inside playing Uno by candlelight like normal people, not out carousing the streets in our ogre truck."

"Monster truck."

"Whatever." The truck lumbered past as William shook his head. "They're probably looters."

"Please. We don't have looters."

"Really? We don't have ogres, either, but there they go down Sixth Street," William said, and blew out of mouthful of smoke.

CHAPTER

EIGHTEEN

S o what's the deal with Maggie?" Axel asked around a
new cigarette.

Wyatt brought his head in from the passenger
side window, where he'd been checking to see if they
were as high as he felt.

"What do you mean?" he asked.

"You think she just missed the window for getting out
of town, or what?"

"I don't know. That doesn't sit right," Wyatt answered.
"She was ready to hit the road at like six yesterday."

"Trouble with the Jeep, maybe?"

"Maybe."

It could be trouble with the Jeep, combined with a hurricane, and added to a lack of cell service. That was all just
a little too coincidental for Wyatt, though he really didn't
have any concrete ideas otherwise.

He looked out the windshield and got the sensation that
he was coming in for a landing. It made him a little quea-
sy, so he looked back out the window.

"How's she been doing? You know, since David."

"She's doing okay," Wyatt said after a moment. "They're doing okay."

"I haven't seen her since the funeral, but I really don't know what to say, man," Axel said. "I'm not that great at meaningful conversation."

Wyatt turned and looked at Axel. "You guys were really close, right?"

Axel glanced over at him. "Me and David? Yeah, best friends since junior high."

"Is that why you and Maggie never dated?"

"Me? And Maggie? No, man," Axel said. "She was beautiful—still is, but I try to go for the least compatible match I can find. Besides, she and David were together forever."

"Since her christening. Yeah, I know."

Axel looked over at him and grinned. "Kind of intimidating, isn't it?"

Wyatt frowned at him. "How do you mean?"

"Geez, Wyatt. You guys don't really think it's *that* much of a secret, do you?" He smiled as Wyatt tried to look confused. "I mean, it's not in your face obvious, but it's not all that hard to see, either."

"We're not dating, if that's what you're implying."

"I'm not implying crap, I'm saying you guys have something going on."

"We work together," Wyatt said, and looked back out the window. "I'm her boss."

"I'm Petey's boss, too, but we don't actually try real hard to look like we're not seeing each other, you know what I mean?" Axel tossed his cigarette out the window. "Besides, David told me."

Wyatt sighed and looked over at Axel.

"Hey, he was okay with it," Axel said. "As okay as you could expect, anyway. He liked you."

"I liked him, too. I really did," Wyatt said. "But, it's against Sheriff's Office policy."

Axel shrugged. "Well, I'm against policies."

"Then you'll understand if I ask you not to tell anybody about it, right?"

"Don't sweat it," Axel answered, lighting another cigarette. "I don't actually like to talk to people."

⚓ ⚓ ⚓

Boudreaux sort of crouched in the water, leaning his head against the trunk of a very young oak. He'd told Maggie he needed to stop and rest a moment, but he suspected that she did, as well.

He turned his head and looked at her. She had an arm wrapped around the tree, and had laid her forehead against the trunk and closed her eyes.

He was struck, as he often had been over the years, by how much she favored her mother. He couldn't see anything physical of himself in her, but over the last couple of months, he had come to see that, as far as her personality, she did resemble him somewhat.

She was strong and she was direct, she had a very dry sense of humor, and she was fiercely protective of those she loved. He knew that she could push herself past the point at which she became afraid, and that she didn't become close to people easily.

He supposed that some of these things could be attributed to some of her experiences, as both a teenager and a cop. But he liked to think that at least some of it was genetic.

She opened her eyes and looked right at him, not even a foot away, and he almost felt as though she'd heard him thinking.

"How old is Miss Evangeline?" she asked him.

It took him a moment to understand what she'd asked him. "I have no idea," he said. "Almost a hundred. Why?"

"She's really important to you, isn't she?"

Boudreaux stared at her a moment. He felt a shaking in his chest, a fluttering like a small bird in a very large, otherwise empty space, and he noticed that the tingling sensation that had been in his feet had also now started in his hands. It felt a lot like fainting without falling down.

"It occurred to me not too long ago that she's the only woman I've ever loved," he said finally.

Maggie blinked at him a few times. "You've never been in love?"

"No." *No, I apologize. Not even with your mother. I didn't even know your mother.*

"That's sad."

"I suppose it is," he admitted. "But it's also probably just as well."

He turned around, put his forehead against the tree and grabbed it with both hands.

"Miss Evangeline is going to be quite put out with me," he said, though he wanted to say something important, something he would want her to remember.

"Why? Because you ruined your shirt?"

He tried to smile at her, but he was losing his peripheral vision. "Something of that nature."

"Come on, we need to get moving again," she said.

He turned back around to face the direction they'd been heading, but he found it too tiresome to actually push away from the tree. "How much further to your house?" he asked her.

"Not far, maybe a hundred yards or so, to those evergreens, then once we get around those, we'll be behind my chicken house."

"Okay. Lead the way," he said in a near whisper, though he couldn't see the evergreens, or her for that matter.

Maggie turned and waded a few steps, then looked over her shoulder as Boudreaux slipped sideways into the water.

She turned around and sloshed her way back to him, reached down and grabbed his shirt collar with both hands and pulled his head back out of the water.

"Stop it!" she yelled stupidly. She got one arm under one of his and tried to pull him upright. "Boudreaux!"

His eyelids didn't even flutter, and she couldn't tell for certain if he was even breathing. She put two fingers of her free hand to his neck, and thought she might feel something, but it was hard to hold him still, and her hand was shaking.

She looked back over her shoulder toward the house. She'd been cursing the flood water, but now she wished there were just a little bit more of it. It wasn't deep enough to swim, and swimming him back would be so much easier.

She looked around hurriedly for something she might be able to float him on, but there was nothing. Just water and bushes and trees. She put her fingers on his lower lip and pulled his mouth open, put her ear next to it. She was pretty sure she couldn't feel or hear any breath, but she was also pretty sure she wasn't sure. At least, not sure enough to leave him there. There was also no way to do CPR in the damn water, at least not that she knew.

She stared at him a second, then reached underwater with her free hand and grabbed at his belt. It took her a minute to get it undone and then pull it out of the belt loops, but she finally yanked it up out of the water.

She pulled it across his chest and pulled each end under his arms, then held on as she moved behind him. She buckled it as close as she could to his upper back, then she

grabbed onto the buckle, turned around, and started wading.

CHAPTER

NINETEEN

W yatt tried not to hold his breath as Axel's truck
tires rolled over yet another bony pine tree lying
across Bluff Road.

They'd been climbing over trees for the last
hour it seemed, and Wyatt's hip was screaming from all
of the jolting. He supposed driving four hours and wading
around downtown might have contributed as well, but he
mostly blamed Axel's ridiculous truck.

Once the back tires rolled over the tree, Wyatt leaned
his head against the window jamb. Axel looked over at
him.

"You're not getting seasick or anything are you there,
Wyatt?"

"No. It's the damn hip. I think it might have come
loose."

He had a sudden vision of himself climbing down out of
Axel's truck and falling to the ground, his left leg missing
and inexplicably naked, like an unwanted Ken doll.

"Hey, look at the bright side, man," Axel said. "You might qualify for a discount on one of those Hoveround things."

Wyatt tossed him a look. "You're adorable. I can't imagine why you get divorced so frequently."

"Yeah, I'm a real enigma," Axel said back.

⚓ ⚓ ⚓

Sky and Kyle had left the window seat only to use the restroom, get a bottle of water, or take turns wiping up rooster poop.

After a while, Kyle had leaned against one side of the window and nodded off, and Sky was left alone, and able to stop trying so hard to look or sound hopeful. She had no idea how long it had been since she'd watched the truck slide past the chicken house with her mother's body sprawled in the back of it, but it had been a long time.

It was still raining but not nearly as hard, and she had been able for the last little while to see most of the yard pretty clearly. She had stared through the trees until she was sure she saw something every time she blinked.

She had stared at the chicken house, or what was left of it after the roof had blown away, waiting for her mom to come to around the corner, but she'd never materialized. For the last several minutes, Sky had been planning what she could say to Kyle when he woke up, to keep him from getting too discouraged. She had even started seeing the two of them in her head, moving into Grandma and Granddad's guest room when their mother failed to return.

She rubbed at her eyes and gave herself a good mental shaking, then reached out and scratched at Coco's jaw when the dog started whining. Then she got up and went to look for something to eat, more to occupy her mind than to fill her stomach.

She was halfway to the kitchen when she heard Coco let out a sound that was half baying wolf and half dying lawnmower. Sky turned around as Coco scrambled up onto the window seat and started pawing at the window.

Sky ran back over, as Kyle sat up and looked around, then looked out the window. They spotted her at the same time.

"Mom!" Kyle yelled.

⚓ ⚓ ⚓

Maggie had just cleared the trees beside the chicken house and waded into the open when she heard the slightly muffled sounds of Coco going berserk. The sound was almost too joyful, too welcoming for Maggie to bear, and something like a balloon came up from her chest and out of her mouth, sounding half sob and half laughter.

She looked up toward the house as Coco continued to call out to her, and tried to smile. "I'm trying," she said, but she was so out of breath that even she could barely hear it.

Her right arm was numb and yet shaking violently, and she stopped to turn around and change the hand that gripped Boudreaux's belt. Then she trudged on, at least feeling a new strength in her legs.

She focused on the area of water just in front of her, made herself not look at how far she had to go yet, even though it really wasn't that far at all.

Then she heard Coco barking, and it was much louder and clearer, and when Maggie looked up, she saw Coco running back and forth on the side deck, saw her two children, saw Sky doing something at the rail, and then realized that her daughter was throwing the rope ladder over the side.

Maggie almost cried from the sight of it, but then she turned and looked at Boudreaux, and looked back up at Sky with resignation. She wanted to call up to her, but she just didn't have the air. But then she saw Sky look beyond her to Boudreaux, and seconds later the girl was over the rail and climbing down the ladder.

Maggie wanted to yell at her not to come down, but she couldn't do that, either. Instead, she just watched, hanging onto Boudreaux's belt buckle, as Sky almost ran through the water, calling out to her.

"Mom!" she yelled one last time as she threw her arms around her Maggie's neck. The force of it almost knocked Maggie down. She wrapped her free arm around Sky's back, buried her face in her hair, but she found she couldn't say anything at that moment. She thought so much—so much—but couldn't say any of it until Sky pulled away and looked down at Boudreaux.

"Is he dead?" Sky asked.

"I don't know," Maggie managed. "But I can't get him up there."

Sky spun around, looked around the yard and then turned back to Maggie. "Here, give him to me," she said, and reached down and snatched at the belt buckle. Maggie let her take it.

"Come on," Sky said, grabbing Maggie's wrist with her free hand.

She pulled Maggie toward the driveway, and Maggie noticed David's old Toyota truck, submerged almost to the tops of the tires, but only about three feet closer to the house than it had been when Sky had parked it the day before. It was then that Maggie realized that Sky had parked right in front of the pile of gravel that Gray had brought to widen the driveway. The truck must have been pushed up against it instead of being carried away.

They made their way over to the back of the truck, and Sky reached up and pulled down the tailgate. It was a few inches above the surface of the water, but Sky turned around and shoved her arms underneath Boudreaux's.

"Grab his legs," she said to Maggie, and Maggie reached under the water and took hold of Boudreaux's calves. It took two tries, but they finally slid him on to the bed of the truck. He landed with a wet thump, and Maggie looked for signs of pain or discomfort on his face but saw none.

"Do you have a beach blanket or anything in the truck?" she asked Sky.

"No. Wait," she said, and spun around and ran to the cab as Maggie picked up one of Boudreaux's wrists and felt for a pulse. She thought she felt one, a very weak one, but her own heart was pounding so hard, and her hand shaking so much, that she wasn't certain of it.

Sky came running back with a bundle in her hands, and Maggie's chest ached when she saw that it was one of the tarps David had used to cover his lap during culling when he sometimes went oystering.

She pushed the thought from her mind and took the tarp, then climbed up into the bed of the truck. She wanted to cover Boudreaux's face to shield it from the rain, but that would be too much like covering a body, so she spread it over him and tucked it underneath his shoulders and legs.

"Mom, we need to get you inside," Sky said, and Maggie turned around to look at her.

"I can't just leave him out here, Sky."

"Yes, you can. You're bleeding."

"Where?" Maggie asked, reaching up to feel her nose.

"The back of your head, Mom."

Maggie reached up and placed a palm to her head, but she'd been wet for forever. If she was bleeding, she couldn't feel it. But when she brought her hand back, it was red.

"Oh," she said quietly. "Wow."

Sky reached out and took her mother's bloody hand and pulled. "Come on."

Maggie slid back out of the truck bed and into the water, and she and Sky made their way to the rope ladder. Maggie was to go up first, and when she looked up at it, Kyle was leaning over the rail, staring down at her. He was soaked anyway, but she could tell that he was crying.

She took a deep breath, then climbed the ladder, which seemed twice as long as it should have. When she got level with the deck rail, she grabbed onto it and threw a leg over. Kyle grabbed her upper arms and helped her get over the rail, and Maggie sat down hard on the deck floor. Then, without planning to, she collapsed onto her back, wishing that she hadn't as soon as her head connected with the wood.

Kyle knelt down beside her and she pulled him down with one arm, clutched him to her and buried her face in his hair as he laid on her chest. Coco bounced from one side of them to the other, then flopped onto her side next to Maggie and furiously licked her face.

Over Kyle's shoulder, Maggie saw Sky vault over the deck rail, and it was at that moment that Maggie felt like she could breathe again. They were all out of the water.

As Sky knelt down next to her on her right, Maggie's eye caught movement to her left and she turned her head. Stoopid was standing there, and even though the rain was falling almost softly now, he hated any form of precipitation, and Maggie was touched that he'd braved it to come out and give her the one-eyed rooster stare.

He emitted a couple of his hen-like *brrps,* updating her that he was stuck upstairs, or out of grit, or that they'd been having some weather.

"I know already," she said quietly, and he shook the rain from his feathers, put his wings partway out, and tapped away awkwardly, looking like a day-old paper airplane.

TWENTY

A short time later, Maggie sat on the edge of the old trunk they used as a coffee table, in dry yoga pants and a sweater, holding a wet cloth to the back of her head.

She had drunk two bottles of water, thrown one up, and was trying to drink another when she heard something outside, and Sky and Coco jumped up together to go look.

Sky opened the front door and just stood there for a moment. "Dude," she said finally.

Maggie got to her feet with some effort and followed Kyle over to the door.

"Whoa," Kyle said softly.

Maggie looked over his shoulder, and watched as the biggest, bluest truck she'd ever seen pulled into the front yard, on tires that were taller than she was.

It stopped in front of the house, and they walked out onto the front deck. Maggie was still trying to figure out who was driving when Wyatt stuck his head out the passenger window.

"Where the hell are your stairs?"

Sky pointed toward the side deck. "There's a ladder," she called down.

Wyatt pulled his head back in and the truck backed up, turned around, and then slowly backed up to the gaping opening where Maggie's stairs used to be. The bed of the truck couldn't have been more than a foot below the deck.

When it stopped, Axel Blackwell opened the driver's side door and stepped out onto the running board.

"I don't need your damn stairs," Axel said. "You look pretty crappy there, Maggie."

"Thanks, Axel," she said.

The passenger door swung open, and after a moment, Wyatt slowly stepped onto his own running board, grabbed onto the side of the truck bed, and gingerly turned to face her. His thick brows scrunched together as he looked up at Maggie.

"What the hell happened?" he demanded.

"Pretty much everything," she said weakly. She pulled the washcloth down from her head and swallowed as she saw it was pretty well bloodied.

"What the *hell*, Maggie?" Wyatt yelled. "We need to get you to the hospital."

Maggie nodded, and Axel waved his arm at the bed of the truck.

"Climb in. Let's go!" he called.

"Go, Sky," Maggie said, then turned around to Kyle, as Sky jumped down into the back. "Kyle, make sure Stoopid has food and water and shut the door."

"He's crapped like all over the planet," Kyle said.

Maggie ignored the language for a change and shook her head. "Put him inside, please."

He hurried back inside, and Maggie watched as Axel held a hand out to Sky. "Come on, Sky, climb down here and get inside."

Maggie looked over at Wyatt. She wasn't sure if he looked scared or just angry. He looked a lot of things.

"Can you get down?" Axel called to her after he'd helped Sky into the cab.

Maggie nodded as she heard Kyle's footsteps behind her. "Yes, but take Kyle first," she said. "Go on, Kyle."

Kyle jumped down into the truck, and Maggie watched until he was in the cab, then she tossed the washcloth and grabbed the deck rail before jumping down into the back. Then she turned around and looked at Coco, who was waiting on the deck.

"Come on, baby," Maggie said. Coco's eyebrows wrinkled with concern, but after a little toe tapping, she jumped in beside Maggie. Maggie turned and looked at Axel. "We have to get Boudreaux."

"Boudreaux where?" Axel asked.

"Boudreaux!?" Wyatt yelled simultaneously.

"He's in the back of David's truck," Maggie said to Axel. Axel looked over that way, then climbed back into his seat.

She looked at Wyatt and saw his shoulders slump as he dropped his head. Then he looked back up at her, and he looked unhappy.

"Freakin' Boudreaux," he said.

Maggie could hear Axel saying something in the cab, and Wyatt ducked down a bit to look inside.

"Just go," he yelled, then straightened up and looked at Maggie. "Sit down."

Maggie got onto her knees, and Wyatt held onto the side of the truck bed as Axel pulled alongside the Toyota, then pulled behind it, tailgate to tailgate, with a significant height difference. Boudreaux was just as Maggie and Sky had left him.

Wyatt leaned over and looked down at Boudreaux, then back over at Maggie. "What did you do to him?"

"Nothing. It was the storm."

"Is he dead?"

"I don't know."

Axel's door opened and he and Sky jumped out into the water. Maggie put a hand on the tailgate, intending to climb into the back of the Toyota, but Wyatt pointed at her.

"Not you!" he barked.

Maggie stopped, and watched Axel and Sky open the back of the Toyota, climb in and reach for Boudreaux. They worked together to scoot him toward the larger truck, then Axel opened his tailgate and they lifted him up and slid him in.

"Yeah, we gotta go," Axel said as he slammed the tailgate shut.

"There's room in here, climb in," Wyatt said behind Maggie.

She turned and looked at him, then shook her head. "I'll ride in back with Coco."

He frowned at her, but she sat down and pulled Coco to her. He sighed and slowly pulled himself back into the cab.

⚓　⚓　⚓

William was sitting at the white wrought iron table on the balcony, smoking a cigarette and trying to find the number for the insurance company, when he heard the rumbling from down the street.

He leaned over to try to see up the block, but ended up having to stand and go to the railing. He looked out and blew a cloud of smoke out in an excited puff.

"Robert!" he called out. "The looters are back!"

Robert appeared behind him, two glasses of tea in hand, just as the behemoth crawled through the intersection and passed below.

The two men stared down into the truck bed.

"It's the little sheriff," William gasped. "And a hyena."

"And a dead guy," Robert said.

William sighed. "Of course she's got a dead guy. What else would she be riding around with?"

"Did you get the insurance company's number?"

"No, let's just move back to Fort Lauderdale, already," William said. "I am up to *here* with living in Mystic Falls."

⚓ ⚓ ⚓

Deputy Dwight Shultz turned onto Avenue D and coasted through the water. He'd been coming out of the parking lot at Weems Memorial when he met Axel and them pulling in. After a few terse explanations from Wyatt, Maggie had asked Dwight to drive over to Boudreaux's.

He turned into the oyster shell driveway and shut off the cruiser, then opened the door and stepped out, his black rain boots splashing softly into the water.

He shut the door, then started up the walkway toward the front porch. Halfway there, he looked up and stopped short.

There was a miniature little old lady standing on the porch with a walker, her head poking out of an enormous black trash bag. When he looked her in the face to say something to her, he saw that there were tears rolling down her wrinkled brown cheeks.

TWENTY-ONE

little less than twenty-four hours later, Maggie woke up from a nap to see Wyatt sitting in the ugly green vinyl chair next to her bed, as he had been when she'd gone to sleep a few hours earlier. As he had been all night.

He was reading a James Lee Burke book, with a pair of reading glasses pushed up onto his head uselessly.

"Hey," Maggie said.

"Hey," he said without looking up.

She waited a moment, but he just kept reading.

"Are you not looking at me?" she asked him finally.

"No, I'm not speaking to you," he said to his book.

"You were speaking to me last night."

"That was last night. Last night I was relieved. Now I'm just pissed."

"What for?" she asked sharply, grabbing onto the bed rail.

The corners of his mouth turned down as he thought about that, then he stuck his finger inside the book to mark his place before he closed it and looked up at her.

"I'm not sure. Probably because you scared the crap out of me."

"This wasn't exactly my fault," she said.

"No, but I don't have anyone else to get mad at that isn't dead already."

She tried not to smile. "How long are you going to be mad?"

He stood up and put his much larger hand on top of hers. "Until I'm not."

She smiled up at him, but he pulled his eyebrows together.

"Where are the kids?"

"They were beat. Your Mom took them back to her house."

"Where's Daddy?"

"Out counseling your rooster." He sighed when Maggie looked at him questioningly. "He went out there to take Stoopid some grit and check on the chickens."

Maggie smiled and nodded. "Okay."

He looked at her for a few moments, his face growing serious. "I was pretty scared," he said finally.

"Me, too," Maggie answered.

"Let's avoid fear for a while."

"Okay."

⚓ ⚓ ⚓

Gray walked down the hallway, his deck shoes soundless on the tile floor. He kept his eyes on the right-hand wall, checking the numbers on the little black plaques as he went. Finally, he saw 202 and knocked twice, then gently pushed open the door.

The curtains were closed and the room was dim, with the only light coming from the partially-open doorway.

It took a moment for his eyes to adjust, then he stepped around the partition and walked over to the bed.

Boudreaux was raised up into a semi-seated position, with an IV in the back of his left hand, and a couple of monitors beeping behind him.

He opened his eyes as Gray stopped beside the bed and put his hands on the rail. His face was expressionless, and he didn't speak. Gray swallowed, then cleared his throat.

"I hear your surgery went well," he said quietly.

Boudreaux nodded slightly. "Yes," he said, his voice hoarse and low.

Gray nodded back, then stared at the bed, somewhere around Boudreaux's knees, for a long moment. Then he looked back up at Boudreaux.

"Well," he said, and stuck out his hand.

Boudreaux took it and they shook. Gray nodded once more, then walked back out of the room and let the door close softly behind him.

He walked a few doors down, then opened the door to Room 209 and stepped inside.

Wyatt was standing by the bed, and he and Maggie both looked at Gray as he walked up to the foot of the bed.

"Hey, Sunshine," he said to Maggie.

"Hey, Daddy," she said, smiling.

Gray looked at Wyatt. "I've come to relieve you so you can go downstairs and get that X-ray."

Maggie looked at Wyatt. "You need another X-ray?"

Wyatt sighed. "It's fine. Dr. Hamilton's just punishing me."

"That's bull," she said. "You messed up your hip, didn't you?"

"No, I'm coming along nicely, thank you."

Gray reached over and slapped Wyatt on the shoulder. "Go on, before he decides you need a colonoscopy, too."

Wyatt gave him a look, then stared at him for a moment.

"What?" Gray asked.

"I'm going to kiss your daughter," he said.

"Well, just don't be sloppy about it."

Wyatt bent down and kissed Maggie lightly, then gave her a kiss on the forehead for good measure.

"How was that?"

"Neat enough," Gray said.

Wyatt patted Maggie's hand goodbye, and when he had left the room, Gray took his place beside the bed, leaned down and kissed the top of Maggie's head.

"How are the chickens?" she asked him.

"They're good. It's still too wet to move them back to the yard, but they'll be okay in the shed for one more night."

"And Stoopid?"

"He's about how you'd expect. He's not loving Clancy's old dog crate."

Maggie smiled, then reached up and took Gray's hand.

"Thanks, Daddy. I appreciate it."

He squeezed her hand gently.

"Anything for my little girl."

⚓   ⚓   ⚓

Two days later Boudreaux sat in the vinyl arm chair by his window, watching as county workers trimmed some damaged trees across the street. Everything was still wet, but the water itself was gone, and everyone was working to make it seem like Faye hadn't happened.

He looked away from the window as he heard his door swish open, and Maggie walked around the partition.

She was wearing jeans and a flowered blouse, and the bandage on her head was gone.

"Mr. Boudreaux," she said when she'd reached his chair.

"Maggie," he said quietly.

She smiled at him a little. "You're up."

"Yes, they've decided I can be trusted to sit in a plastic chair without harming myself."

She looked at him for a moment. "I'm not really surprised to see you've had some better clothes brought in."

Boudreaux looked down at his silk robe. "Yes. I see you're dressed as well."

"Yes. I'm going home."

He nodded. "Good. I'm glad that you're recovering well."

"Hard heads run in my family."

He blinked at her, then gave her half a smile.

"Anyway, I just came in to thank you again."

He put a hand on either arm of the chair and gently pushed himself up, then stood. "That's really not necessary," he said as he slowly walked over to the little plastic table by his bed and picked up a book.

"Thank you for the reading material. I enjoyed it."

He walked over and held the book out to her, the James Lee Burke that Wyatt had been reading.

She took it, then looked at him for a moment. She seemed a bit uncomfortable.

"What is it, Maggie?"

She gently let out a breath before she answered. "I was thinking that I'd like to hug you goodbye."

He looked at her for a moment, then swallowed and held out one arm. She stepped closer, and tentatively put her arms around his neck. He closed his arm around her waist, and he could smell coconut shampoo in her hair as he lowered his head next to hers. He breathed it in soundlessly, then put his other arm around her and held her.

As they stood there, he realized that it was the first time, the only time, that he had held his only child.

Then she stepped back and looked into his eyes and gave him a polite smile.

"Goodbye, Mr. Boudreaux."

"Goodbye, Maggie," he said.

Then he watched her turn and walk out of the room.

THE END

Look for the fifth book in the *Forgotten Coast Florida Suspense Series*, coming to Amazon November 2015.

GET UNFORGOTTEN

T o get UnForgotten, and be the first to hear about new releases, special 99-cent pricing for friends of the series, and fun news about the books and Apalach, please subscribe to the newsletter.

I'd like to extend a special thank you to so many of you who have taken the time to send me an email or post on my Facebook page. I truly love hearing from my readers, and your enthusiasm and support has been incredibly encouraging to me.

As always, your honest review would be deeply appreciated. If you could take a moment to share your experience with *Landfall*, I would be thrilled. Also, feel free to drop me a line anytime, at dawnmckenna63@gmail.com

Thank you all!
Dawn Lee

ACKNOWLEDGEMENTS

Thank you to Tammi Labrecque, of LarksandKatydids, for her tireless editing efforts, hilarious comments, and constant encouragement.

Thanks to Colleen Sheehan of Write.Dream.Repeat for her beautiful book designs and high tolerance for my ADD.

To Shayne Rutherford of DarkMoonGraphics, thank you so much for your beautiful covers. They are truly the perfect designs for this series.

To my fellow patients at Author's Corner; your support, assistance, hilarity, encouragement, experience and friendship have been and will always be among the things for which I am so grateful.

And to my family: all of you are the reasons that I write, and all of you are the reasons that I can. I love you something stupid.

CPSIA information can be obtained
at www.ICGtesting.com
Printed in the USA
LVHW040155030519
616492LV00005B/78